THE STRANGE
THING WE BECOME
AND
OTHER DARK TALES

Eric LaRocca

For Lynn

(8 March 1943 - 2 May 2010)

"No one dies who is remembered."

TABLE OF CONTENTS

YOU FOLLOW WHEREVER THEY GO

"WHY DON'T YOU GO OUT there and introduce yourself?" he asks me with a charm I had forgotten he possessed—a grin so cloying that a magician might redden.

My eyes drift out the rain-spattered window, watching the group of children crowd near the entrance to our driveway—a coterie of adolescents wearing dark-colored costumes made of papier-mâché and toting bright Chinese lanterns.

Some of the group members carry large percussive instruments like hand drums, brass cymbals, and tambourines. They float down the center of the empty lane just beyond where the house lights reach as if they were a flock of blackbirds.

"They wouldn't like me," I say, chewing on my lip until it turns purple.

My father isn't convinced.

"They seem pleasant enough," he says, straining to wave at them before exhaustion has its arms around him and pulls him down on an invisible leash.

They don't seem to notice my father as they mill about near our mailbox, clanging their instruments like a horse's hooves

1

beating against cobblestones.

"How do you know?" I ask, just to be smart.

"Well, don't they?"

One of the older boys in the group steers the front of the small band, hands fluttering wildly as he conducts their makeshift symphony.

"Seems odd for them to rehearse in the rain like this," I say. Never mind the fact we had moved to Saint Benedict—a small town in the northeastern corner of New Hampshire—nearly three weeks ago and hadn't seen any children in the neighborhood until now.

"Go on," my father insists, coughing slightly and smearing threads of saliva across his mouth as he hunts in the kitchen cupboard for a flashlight.

He finds one with a cracked handle and passes it to me.

"I wasn't invited."

My father's shoulders drop. His voice softens—brittle thin as if the small tumor in his brain were speaking for him. "You don't need an invitation."

"I'll get soaked."

He's already rummaging in the coat closet near the front door, dragging out an umbrella printed with a collection of ladybugs. "Here. Borrow the umbrella."

I think of another excuse. Anything to get out of this. "My boots have holes in them."

"Borrow mine," he says, pointing at the mud-slimed galoshes in the boot basket beside the foyer's credenza.

I cross my arms like a petulant toddler. "They don't fit me right."

"You'll only be wearing them for a few minutes," he reminds me, ushering me from the dining room into the foyer. "Just go out there and say 'hello.'"

"They'll laugh at the way I say things," I say, covering my mouth as if it were an attempt to hide my lisp.

"They won't."

"You don't know for sure."

"Not everybody in this world is out to hurt you," he says.

If anybody had a right to complain about unfair treatment, it would be him.

"You don't know that."

"I've never hurt you," he reminds me with a gentle hand around my shoulder.

"Parents aren't supposed to hurt their children."

His head lowers as if in prayer. "Sometimes they do."

My attention returns to the small group of children gathered on the street, idling there as if waiting for something—a sign, a warning, anything.

"Will you come with me?" I beg him.

My father laughs until he's hoarse, sliding a hand across his bald head from where the chemotherapy robbed him of his once auburn curls. "You think introducing them to your father will help get you on their good side?"

"They won't mind."

He draws in sharply, considering his every word. "Sometimes you have to do things on your own."

For the first time in thirteen years, I'm honest with him. "I'm scared," I say.

"I'll be right here watching you."

But I'm too stubborn for my own good. "You can't come with me?"

"I can't be with you all the time," he says, deflating as if he knows full well how much he's hurting me. "We've already talked about this."

The thought arrives in my mind like an unwelcome guest— an unannounced visitor barreling through the front door and setting fire to the living room rug. "What if they ask me to go with them?"

"Follow them," he says. "You're allowed."

"Wherever they go?"

"Of course."

I know just how to hurt him—how to curl an invisible hand inside him like radiation's fingers. "You just want me gone," I say.

I instantly regret it. He doesn't deserve to be hurt. Besides, I've already done enough harm to him.

"You know that's not true," he tells me. Voice thinning to a whisper, he eases himself into one of the only small chairs in the foyer not piled with unopened cardboard boxes. "It's just—I'm worried. Have been for a while."

"Yes?"

"I'm worried you won't be able to take care of yourself when I'm gone."

Once again, another obscene thought crashes into my mind and violently roots itself where I can't pluck it away—the thought of my father, his face pallid and ashen, framed inside a wooden pine box and being carried away by well-dressed pallbearers.

"But you're not leaving anytime soon. Right?"

He caresses my hand. "You have a child to give them to the world. Not keep them from it."

"Is that what you're doing?" I ask. "Giving me to the world?"

"You'll see one day," he says. "When you have a family of your own."

I can't even entertain the thought. "I won't," I say. "I won't ever be without you."

His eyes lower for a moment. Then, they meander out the window, staring blankly at the small band of children idling beside our mailbox and quietly playing their instruments as a rain shower beats against them.

"You know," he says, "in some countries they bind children's feet to keep them as tiny and as delicate as possible."

"I know," I say, cringing slightly as I recall the black-and-white photographs I've seen in history class.

"Well," he says, "you can either wear shoes too small for you. Or you can find shoes your own size."

He stretches out his hand, passing the flashlight to me.

I consider it for a moment.

Do I dare?

Then, as if commanded by a bloodless worm twitching in my brain, I snatch the flashlight from his hands. I shove my feet into my father's pair of rainboots; my toes curling at the smallness of their size.

I peck my father with a kiss on his forehead. His skin feels warm as if feverish.

Opening the door and sailing down the front steps, I weave across the lawn as I scale the small embankment leading to the roadway where the band of children waits for me. Rain drizzles, blurring my sight until I smear the water from my eyes.

Greeting them with a halfhearted wave and an unsure smile creasing my face, they lower their percussive instruments, and their playing comes to a halt. The leader of the group—a blonde-haired boy dressed in a gold lamé suit—approaches me.

Out of the corner of my eye, I notice a car suddenly idling in the driveway, an insignia for "Beacon Hospice Care" plastered along the side of the vehicle.

"When did that get here?" I ask.

I turn my head slightly and watch as an ambulance arrives, a dark crimson shadow leeching across the lawn. A body draped in white linen is carried out from the house, medics sliding the corpse into the rear of the vehicle and latching the doors shut.

A breath escapes me with a single word. "Dad?"

The blonde-haired boy in the gold lamé suit inches closer toward me, his followers shadowing him and closing in around me the way a herd of animals surround a wounded member of their pack.

"You look uncomfortable," he says, pitifully.

His eyes scan me from my head to my feet. Then, he kicks off his boots and swipes them from the ground.

"These should be your size," he says, passing them to me.

He sees the confusion on my face, my eyes searching him for an explanation.

He smiles at me. "You're one of us now."

One of the other children elbows their way through the crowd toward me and offers me a tambourine.

"We should be on our way," he says to the group as they prepare their instruments once more.

They begin to march down the lane, clanging their cymbals and skirting beyond the streetlights like small insects. I'm glued to where I'm standing, for a moment too afraid to join. It's not long before a gentle breeze pushes me along as if it were a gentle hand dragging me after them.

The blonde-haired boy passes a paper lantern to me, his eyes seeming to tell me that the place to which we're headed will be dark.

BODIES ARE
FOR BURNING

AS THE IVY LEAGUE STENCH from Dr. Caldwell's breath tickles the hairs in my nostrils, I think of pushing the burning end of a lighter against his mouth just to get him to shut up.

I hate myself for welcoming the thought.

I imagine his lips, as thin as elastic bands, crisping until black and then sprouting open like exploded grapes left all day in sunlight. Of course, I expect him to resist slightly—eyes bulging and searching me for an explanation I cannot divulge. After all, it's an answer I don't understand entirely myself as the truth of my obsession has moored itself in some secret cavern deep inside me—the urge to burn things.

The relentless pageant of obscenities continues to filter throughout my mind, each thought armored with needle-sharp spindles and carried by a parade of centipede feet. I imagine the next of my many labors as I think of holding a match inside his left nostril—thistles of black hair sizzling hot and tissue blistering red until every hole in his face releases a dim cloud of smoke. When his nose resembles the remains of a half-melted candle—an ivory fang of cartilage fixed in the outlet at the center of his

6

grotesquely misshapen face—I imagine setting my sights on the last tokens I'll take from him: his eyes.

I pretend I can almost hear the agony rattling in the pit of his fear-clogged throat as I think of pressing the lighter against the center of his pupil. I envision his torment, eyelids furiously opening and closing over a mushroomed bulb of tissue oozing like an egg yolk after it's been stamped out with a cigarette. I think to look away, but I'm far too enchanted by the finesse of my craftsmanship.

Just as I'm about to conjure another barbed thought, I notice Dr. Caldwell has stopped speaking and he's instead gawking at me with a look of puzzlement. I'm pulled out of the deep recesses of my mind, and I realize my jaw is hanging open, an annoyingly bemused expression probably making its home across my face from my daydreaming.

"Well—?" he says, prompting me to answer a question I did not hear.

I clear the catch in my throat, shifting uncomfortably inside the prison of his office's upholstered leather armchair.

"Sorry," I say, suddenly very concerned he can see each one of my indecent thoughts as if they were beetles scurrying across my forehead.

He repeats himself: "Tell me about the first time you thought of burning something."

Naturally, I had expected the question. Despite my preparedness, I find myself retreating deep inside my mind as if to locate the words I had rehearsed long ago for such an occasion. They don't come easily at first, each letter of every word clinging to the corners of my mouth before my breath pushes them from my tongue.

"When I was little, I used to think something wasn't yours until you bled on it," I say. I can't believe I've said it. Especially so matter-of-factly. I had expected to come apart, as if uttering the very words would undo the integrity of my entire being.

I'm surprised, and equally thankful, to still remain intact, so I continue. "I used to prick my fingers and dab a small drop of my blood on everything in my room. Everything I wanted to be mine."

My eyes comb his face for a reaction—an eyebrow raised in bewilderment, a lip pulling downward in disapproval. I'm instead met with the distinguished poise of an oil portrait—so stoic it was as if he were posing for an illustrator, his eyes dull and listless.

I'm not sure how, but I convince myself to keep speaking.

"I was maybe . . . eight or nine, and a new girl named Charlotte Watkins had moved to our town," I say, the words slowing as I exhale her name. "I had never felt what I felt for Charlotte before. It surprised me. Scared me, too. I didn't know what it meant at the time. But I know what it means now. I wanted her in a way that would make her belong to me."

I find myself hunching over, as if each syllable of every word were a cinder block being piled upon my spine.

"One day after school, I walked up to her with a piece of paper and asked her to sign her name. She used to sing in the school choir and all the teachers told her she'd be a famous singer one day. So, I told her I wanted her signature for when she was famous."

I take a long pause, excessive enough in length to make Dr. Caldwell visibly uncomfortable, and I watch him squirm like a pinned snake.

"Is that why you wanted her signature?" he asks.

"No," I say. "I took the piece of paper home. I cut my hand open and dripped blood from the wound onto the paper."

I steal another moment to search his face for any semblance of a reaction. He has the reverent look of a disciple in an encaustic portrait well practiced—his narrow eyelids, lips without movement, hands cupped and fixed together in his lap.

"What did you do then?" he asks me.

"It's not what I did. It's what she did to me," I say. I'm unrestrained now. I feel color pooling in my cheeks and my voice becoming weighted at the unpleasant recollection. "I went to school the next day, and I overheard her talking with some of the boys in our class. They asked her why she was hanging out with a freak like me. She told them she wasn't my friend. And never would be."

Dr. Caldwell tilts his head at me as if he were studying a dying insect issuing its final spasms inside a petri dish.

"I wanted to burn the paper," I say. "It was the first time I really wanted to burn something."

"And did you, Hailey?" he asks in a way that makes me think he seems to already know the answer.

"No." I hope to have surprised him. "I crumpled it up and hid it inside the attic wall in our house. We moved when I was thirteen, but I wonder if it's still there."

"And that's precisely what I want you to understand," he says. His tone is suddenly light and airy, almost as if it were an insult to the seriousness of the subject matter. "These are merely thoughts. You've never actually acted on any of them."

His sincerity is hardly comforting.

"I know you've been under a great deal of stress," Dr. Caldwell says, crossing his legs and feigning what I imagine to be the most genuine look of concern he can muster from imitating other people. "Ever since you lost Mia, you've been hurting."

I had always found a way to avoid speaking about Mia ever since she passed over a year ago. Her presence at these sessions had dimmed considerably until she had eventually become a mere afterthought; an unwelcome visitor at a somber two-person party. I skirted around the uncomfortable topic of my dead wife with the dexterity of a carpenter ant avoiding a bead of water. More importantly, I would never confess to how I had betrayed her before she passed—how I had convinced her to be cremated, not because "it takes less a toll on the earth" as I had persuaded her, but because I had wanted to watch her burn.

I would never divulge my secret delight as I had watched the gaunt-faced cremator slide my wife's body through the mouth of the furnace—how I peered through the small window and watched the inferno claim her lifeless body, swaddling her with a blanket of flames and then inhaling her whole. It was as if I were watching the mere sticks of kindling she used to burn in the backyard. I figured Dr. Caldwell already thought poorly of me; I certainly never wanted him to think I was a monster.

"These obsessions are perfectly normal," he tells me. "You need to remind yourself there's a difference between thought and action. Thoughts go away when they come to us and we no longer give them value. We distract ourselves."

Out of the corner of my eye, I spy the clock on the wall—the unofficial referee of our back-and-forth. Only five minutes left. I've been keeping something from him for the past forty minutes, but it's slowly creeping up my esophagus and pushing against my gritted teeth. I push it out in one breath: "My sister wants me to look after my niece tomorrow."

Dr. Caldwell doesn't react. He looks at me as if I've merely recited the weekly weather forecast.

"And—?" he says, sliding his glasses to the tip of his nose and leaning them at me.

I didn't think I'd have to spell it out for him. Part of me resents him for even making me say it: "I'm scared."

Dr. Caldwell continues to play dumb. "Of what?"

I swallow my resentment, hoping the color filling my cheeks doesn't betray my poise. "Of thinking something. Doing something horrible."

My heart sinks when I see Dr. Caldwell simper slightly, almost as if he were thinking it was a possibility.

"Have you done something horrible before?" he asks.

I think of Mia and how I was caught somewhere between fascination and revulsion at myself as I watched her dead body burn.

I lie. "No."

"Then, I can guarantee you won't do something horrible tomorrow," he says. "I have the utmost faith in you."

But I don't trust him.

If I were on fire, Dr. Caldwell would probably hand me a candle.

***

Before I can even pry open the door, my older sister Maud is pushing across the threshold and lugging my niece inside a car seat. She's all smiles as she greets me, wiping auburn hair out of her face and wrapping an arm around my waist.

"Sorry we're late," she says, lowering the car seat to the floor and dropping the messenger bag stuffed with diapers and talcum powder from her shoulder. "Traffic on 95."

"That's OK," I assure her. "I was just cleaning."

I toss the towel I'm holding around my neck and clear the dampness from my forehead. I'm not sweating because of work. I'm sweating because I'm terrified to death of what's to come when my sister leaves. I've already spent most of the morning agonizing over each horrible possibility. I sense my face hardening as if it were made of wax, and I realize Maud is staring because I must look uneasy. I swallow hard, my lips creasing in the most unconvincing smile I can imitate. It's enough to convince Maud, as she seems satisfied.

My sister kneels beside the car seat, unbuckling the one-year-old and fussing with the child's embroidered pink hat. "Grace is so excited to spend time with her Auntie Hailey. Isn't that right, Gracie?"

The child responds, cooing—a sweet gurgle emerging from between her spit-threaded lips. Her arms and legs thrash excitedly as if calibrating the efficiency of her motor skills.

I peer out the front door and across the rain-soaked front porch to the vehicle idling in the driveway. I see my sister's mother-in-law dozing, mouth open, in the passenger seat, a hat tilted to one side of her head in a poor effort to conceal her baldness from the chemotherapy.

"How is she?" I ask.

Maud glances back at the idling car, her smile melting at the sight. "She sleeps most of the day. The doctor hopes this will be the last visit."

"How's Jerry?" It's not that I even care. I'm just trying to stall her in order to prevent her from leaving. I dread the moment I'm alone with only my thoughts and the child.

Maud lifts Grace from her car seat, hoisting her against her shoulder and carrying her into the living room. "He's fine. He was asking about you the other day."

I watch the way she cradles her daughter—a hand on the child's bottom and a hand lovingly cupping the nape of her neck. I feel out of place in my own home. It's as if I'm a spectator to a secret ritual passed down from some ancient civilization. The bond of motherhood is something I know I'll never understand.

I watch my sister circle the room, bouncing Grace as she meanders from window to window. She pauses as she gazes into the backyard, eyes squinting, visibly perplexed by the sight of the colossal mound of chopped wood and kindling claiming the lawn as if it were a sleeping giant. My eyes follow hers to the pyramid of brush—a permanent reminder of my wife and all she left unfinished before she had passed.

"One of Mia's projects," I explain.

The excuse doesn't seem to reassure her as she scowls in the way all big sisters seem to know better. "You should have Jerry take care of that."

"Maybe I will," I say in an effort simply to placate her.

Of course, I have no intention of following up with my

11

brother-in-law. It's not because I don't care for him. Quite the contrary. It's simply because I'm afraid of what I'll think of doing to him as he burns the brush pile. I imagine it will involve a scenario I've repeated in my head countless times over—heaving him into the mountain of fire and watching his palsied limbs thrash helplessly as he vanishes into the shimmering inferno.

"Have you thought of selling?" my sister asks me, patting Grace on the back as she rocks her back and forth. "This house is too big for you. Don't you think?"

I feel my chest tightening at the prospect of change. It's as if an electrical current were snaking through my body from my toes to the hairs on my head. After all, I had already betrayed my beloved Mia after she was gone, I certainly couldn't dishonor her memory by selling the house.

"It's not too big," I assure her in a tone that sounds utterly unconvincing, even to me. "Besides, I'm comfortable here. Mia's always with me."

Maud looks at me the way a parent might look at a toddler who says they can't sleep in their room because they've seen a ghost. She shrugs, passing out of the living room and back to the foyer where she delivers Grace to her car seat once more.

"Well, if you're ever interested in selling, let me know. Jerry's friend just got his realtor license."

"Definitely," I say. Another promise I have no intention of fulfilling.

As I watch my sister slip Grace back into the car seat, hurling a blanket across her lap, I find myself staring at the small child, mesmerized. I regard the fullness of her pink cheeks as if her mouth were filled with balls of cotton. I admire her eyes—pools of blue so dark only a sapphire could compare. Finally, I come to her fingers—small, clumsy digits so thin they resemble the stems of flowers.

Suddenly, the thought arrives to me like a canine beckoned by a whistle. I imagine pressing a lighter against the small child's index finger, holding the flame there until her pink skin bursts open and crinkles like a tube of blood sausage. I shake my head as if to fling the disgusting thought from the darkest corner of my brain, but to no avail. Another thought takes its place. This one, more abhorrent than the last. I think of shoving the small child inside the oven and adjusting the temperature dial to 425. I imagine the child's confusion soon giving way to panic as I watch—her puce-colored skin toasting brown and smoke filling the chamber until it draws a black curtain across the glass, and I can only hear the sound of her crying.

Maud must be able to see the sudden panic written across my face because she looks at me queerly.

"Dear—?" she says to me, concerned.

The word snaps me from my daze and I'm returned to the foyer. I see my sister's mouth hanging open as if desperately trying to comprehend, her eyes probing me for an explanation.

"I don't think this is a good idea," I say, opening the front door and hoping my sister will take the hint.

Maud just stands there, staring at me with a look of incredulousness. "Not a good idea? But you said you could watch her."

My speech is clumsy, the words forming in clumps of desperation and panic as my eyes avoid my sister at all costs. "I've just been thinking, and I don't think I can watch Grace. I don't think I can do it."

Maud shakes her head. Folding her arms, she looks as though she had anticipated this. "You always do this," she says. "You always make these commitments you can't keep."

"I don't always—"

"You do. Jerry's sister always makes an effort to see Grace. You never do."

I find myself shrinking away from her, my sister's words reducing me to the size of a thumbtack. She suddenly seems to stifle herself, as if she could sense me hurting the way all sisters are supposed to be bonded by some sort of an invisible tether. It's a fetter I thought had come undone long ago. If it somehow still exists, I imagine it's now secured by the most tenuous of truces.

"I know you've been going through a lot," she says. "I know you're stressed at work."

"Yeah, I may not have a job on Monday," I'm quick to remind her. "They already outsourced the entire tech department."

"I get that you're stressed," she says. "But I asked you for one small favor."

My eyes scour the floor as if I think an explanation for my abruptness will be written there somewhere. I'm met with nothing.

"I thought this would be good for you. You were always talking about how you wanted kids. I thought this would be a nice . . . distraction."

I can't think of anything to say to get out of this. I certainly can't tell her the truth. She'll think I'm a monster.

"Maybe I'm just tired," I say, pretending to rub my eyes. "It'll be fine."

Maud scans me up and down in disbelief. "When I get back, I promise not to bother you again."

Snatching her handbag, Maud sails out the door and down the porch steps toward the car. I watch as she throws herself into the driver's seat and shifts the car into gear, eyes dodging me as she scans the rearview mirror. I wave at her with all the hopelessness of a shipwreck survivor abandoned on a deserted island. Watching her as she retreats down the driveway and slides out onto the roadway, my eyes follow the car until the taillights disappear from view.

It's the moment I had feared the most. I'm finally left alone with the child.

I look at Grace with revulsion as if she were some alien species. I'm too fearful to even go near the car seat at first. I lean closer, testing the child's comfort the same way I might approach a wild animal.

Grace looks at me, not how an infant might reverently observe its mother, but rather how a prisoner regards their captor.

Swallowing my unease, I lift the car seat and ferry Grace into the living room where I've already arranged a small playpen in the corner filled with toys and blankets. Too afraid to even look at her, I glimpse her out of the corner of my eye and see her quizzically studying me the way all infants seem to carefully examine what's foreign to them. Presumably upset by the explanations she must have invented for my presence, Grace's lips start to quiver and she releases soft moans like a wounded animal. I hear a storm churning in the pit of her throat; a scream making its ascent. Before she can utter a sound, I scoop her out of the basket and brace her against my shoulder in a graceless recreation of how my sister had held her.

The child and I make eye contact as I start to bounce her up and down, both of us disturbed by each other's closeness. It feels awkward holding something so precious—something so easy to hurt. My hands are overly cautious, as unsure and as uncoordinated as an amateur sculptor molding clay. Grace's body might as well be made of clay—her every motion a slave to my most indecent whims. The suppleness of her skin squeezing against mine frightens me and thoughts as persistent as blind white maggots swarming carrion begin to worm their way across my mind. I peer across to the dining room and my eyes immediately dart to the two taper candles set on opposite sides of the table.

I imagine lighting one of the candles and tipping the flame against the wiry tufts of hair dotting Grace's head. I think of the sulfurous stench of her follicles as they burn, smoking lines of fire working livid fingers across her scalp. Delighting in the child's bewilderment, I imagine her miming to me in panic as her tiny hands wave at me to no avail. I suddenly realize I'm smiling, my feet somehow carrying me toward the dining room table, and the recognition disgusts me. I stop myself and notice how Grace begins to sag like a concrete brick in my arms, my hands awkwardly straining to keep her from falling. She must sense my uneasiness because she starts to squirm, arms and legs beating against me like a frightened cat pleading to be released.

Before she slips from my grasp, I lean her back into the car seat and retreat—an invisible leash secured between us making it impossible for me to move away more than a few steps. The child fusses for a moment. Then, hugs her blanket, eyelids narrowing to mere slits as if more than content to forget about my clumsiness. But I'm not as easily pacified. I soon sense other equally repulsive thoughts creeping out from the secret crypts within my mind, their fangs exposed and claws unfurling.

Before they can ambush me, my feet sweep me into the kitchen and I'm rummaging through the cabinets in search of a lighter. I grab the only two I can find and toss them in the trash can. The thoughts—with their livid bead-like eyes and their dagger-tipped talons—begin to drain, whirlpooling like oil circling a funnel. I make the most of their resignation, sprinting from room to room and collecting all the candles I can find. When my arms are full, I discard the torches in the trash and heave the black plastic bag out to the sidewalk.

15

As I return to the house, I notice the thoughts—once shrieking like howler monkeys—have now been dimmed to mere whispers. I close my eyes, relishing in the balmy tide of calmness spreading over me. However, it doesn't last long as I soon hear Grace whimpering in the living room. I check on her and am met with a scrunched face, her thin lips creased with a frown so exaggerated she looks as if she were the marionette doll of an elderly woman. She babbles, spouting gibberish as if speaking some sort of extinct dialect and then growing upset when I can't seem to understand her.

After I inspect her diaper for the culprit of her discomfort, I realize she's probably hungry. Sifting through the messenger bag Maud had left, I retrieve a jar of baby formula and a spoon. I lift Grace out of her car seat and drop her into my lap as I uncomfortably arrange myself on the couch. Scooping blended carrots from the jar, I pass some into Grace's mouth and she accepts the food without hesitation. I sense her collapse into me as if reveling in the comfort. I wonder if she mistakes me for her mother. The thought frightens me.

She should be afraid of me.

Just as I'm about to deliver another spoonful to Grace, my eyes narrow at something in the kitchen I had neglected. Something I had forgotten about: the gas stovetop. An open flame. The thought crashes into my mind, stabbing my brain with tendrils armed with needles and hooks. I think of placing Grace's hand on the stovetop and turning the dial until the flame ignites, her tiny fingers swallowed in a bright fiery plume. The more I resist the thought, the more arduously it buries its hooks into me.

A giant hand pulls back a dark curtain from behind my eyes and I suddenly find myself in the kitchen at the stove. Grace slumps in my arms, thrashing as helplessly as a freshly dredged earthworm. My fingers are pinching the wheel, about to twist "ON" when I realize I'm pressing Grace's open palm against the unlit burner. Her eyes—the size of quarters—are wet and shining. Her mouth threaded with spit as sobs gurgle in the shallow hole of her throat. She looks at me panicked and confused; the same way cattle might look while being herded into the slaughterhouse. Although I had once envisioned her bewilderment, nothing could have prepared me for the fear residing in her eyes as she stared at me.

It's not long before I notice the unpleasant thoughts have subsided in my mind, flowering roots plucked from their beds of soil and dragged screaming. I strain to push a thought to the front of my brain, but it's as if I'm playing an instrument that refuses to make a sound. The thought never arrives. Suddenly, I hear the dim sonority of Dr. Caldwell's voice drifting through my eardrum.

"Thoughts go away when they come to us and we no longer give them value," I hear him say. "We distract ourselves."

Yes, a distraction. Sometimes you have to do something horrible to prevent something even worse from happening.

I peer out the kitchen window to the giant pyramid of brush in the backyard, quietly making my plans.

They involve a canister of gasoline and a lighter.

***

After I load Grace into my car, strapping her into the car seat, I peel out of the driveway and sail down the road toward town. Rain beats hard against the windshield, wipers furiously scraping the glass as I drive. I glimpse in my rearview mirror, spying Grace in the backseat as she sits, slumped in her chair and sleeping. I feel pity for her, so cheerfully unaware of the unpleasantness to come.

Even if I had decided to tell her, she wouldn't understand. At least there won't be begging, tearful pleas to spare her or half-gagged supplications promising me everything I could ever dream of. There won't be fear-filled bargaining or, perhaps even most annoying of all, a need for an explanation. Of course, the parents and the police will eventually require answers. But they'll scarcely notice blackened bits of bone in the smoldering remains of a brush pile.

"I forgot I left the back door open," I'll say to them. "I think she crawled out into the yard. I can't believe this happened."

I wonder how I'll actually perform the act when the moment arrives. Naturally I've thought of tossing her on top of the pile when the fire is finally lit and roaring at full blast. But I worry that she'll suffer. Perhaps I'll blindfold her and then crack her head open with a hammer beforehand. No, that won't work either. Too much of a risk with the possibility of blood—a smear of red, my ultimate downfall when the police eventually search my home for her.

I could hold a pillow over her head and then, when I'm certain she's no longer breathing, launch her little body onto the pyramid of brush. But I question my determination to follow through with the ordeal, especially if I'm expected to be physical with her. I wonder if I'll choke and back out at the last second. And then what? Of course, she probably won't remember, but I'll be once again left with my thoughts—as monotonous and as droning as a hive of honeybees.

When I resolve myself to the fact that I'll need to simply get it over with as quickly as possible, I arrive at the store. I scoop Grace out of her seat and lug her into the market, passing through the sliding doors. Scanning the signs hanging above each aisle, I locate the corridor where paper plates, plastic forks, and other picnic supplies are.

I swipe a lighter from the rack, hurling it into my basket and making my way further down the aisle. A young mother with a child strapped to her front in a baby carrier glides past me, smiling as if we both belong to some secret society. I pass a middle-aged man wearing a gray tweed suit; he stalls and admires Grace, cooing at her. She wiggles excitedly, salivating as he kneels to address her.

"Isn't she beautiful?" he says, admiring the child. "Have fun with her."

I nod halfheartedly, faking a polite smile. If only he knew the plans I have in store for her. I'm annoyed at his interruption. I snatch the pink embroidered hat from Grace's head, pocketing it, as if in an effort to render her as unnoticeable as possible. My plan fails immediately, as when I reach the end of the aisle, I'm met by an elderly woman riding on a scooter with a small basket fixed at the bow of the vehicle.

"What a beautiful child," she says, drumming her liver-spot-dotted fingers along the handlebars.

Her tone seems to hint at something else and guilt rakes through me until I split open like an overstuffed purse.

"Thank you," I say, trying to push past her.

But she's too quick for me. The old woman inches forward in her motorized chair, cornering me against the wall.

"She's lucky to have a mother as loving as you in her life," she says.

Then, without another word, the old woman wheels herself

down the aisle and away from me until she's out of eyesight. I stand without movement for a moment, as if every artery within my body had hardened with cement. I hear her words lingering in the air the same way the coppery scent of blood lingers beneath freshly soaped and perfumed skin.

"How could I have been such a monster?" I wonder to myself, even more afraid of the answer.

I look at Grace, disgust ripping apart my insides at the thought of hurting this poor, sweet child. I squeeze her a little closer, as if my gesture were a wordless way to let her know that she's no longer in danger.

I was the danger, after all.

Perhaps I was right. I have to do something horrible to prevent something even worse from happening.

The thought comes to me easily this time. I know what I have to do.

Before another moment of hesitation, I carry Grace out of the store. But not before I pass through the checkout lane to buy a can of gasoline.

***

Rain slows to a trickle when we return home, the sky still dark as if smeared with God's fury. I shovel Grace out of the seat and sprint up the front steps, darting inside the house.

I have so much work to do before Maud gets back. But first, something must be done about Grace.

I tote her back to the living room and set her down in the play pen I've arranged in front of the sliding glass door that opens out to the porch. Passing a stuffed animal into her arms, our hands touch. Her tiny fingers—as delicate and as thin as threads of yarn—brush against mine. Our eyes meet and her mouth crimps slightly with a smile as she hugs her teddy bear.

It feels as if the world slows around us, all noise dimming to a distant hum. I tuck my hand underneath her chin, no longer afraid to touch her.

"When I was with you, I felt like a monster," I say to her. "And I am a monster."

Her stare lingers, quizzically studying me as if trying to decipher my every word.

"But I'm going to leave you alone like a nice monster," I say.

I wrap a blanket across her lap and tuck it in the sides of the car seat so that she can't wiggle free. When I'm finished swaddling Grace, I take a final moment to admire her. She looks peaceful, as if she were floating blindly through a horrible dream. That's exactly how I'd like to remember this—a horrible dream. Luckily, I won't have to remember it for long.

I grab the canister of gasoline, pocketing the matches as I make the trek out to the brush pile in the backyard. The pyramid of splintered wood creaks like a dredged sunken ship. I touch one of the branches. It feels damp and slimy like the skin of an eel.

"This is going to be difficult to burn," I think to myself.

Despite the obvious predicament, I've already made the decision to follow through. Nothing can stop me now. I pop open the canister and sprinkle the brush pile until it's soaked with gas. When the canister is empty, I toss it on the ground and make good use of the matches. I slide a match across the strip and hurl the tiny flame into the brush pile.

I wait a few moments, my breathing suddenly heavier. Watching wisps of smoke drift up from underneath the pyramid, I strike another match and toss it into the pile. Then, I toss another. And another. Angry flecks of orange and yellow flicker beneath the snarling canopy of wood, an inferno about to surface. Smoke billows from the vent fixed at the top of the pile like a chimney. Finally, the fire drags itself out of hiding with mammoth arms, clutching each stick of kindling in its tightening fists. I watch as branches snap and crinkle apart, the wall of flames sweeping across the giant pile as if it were a furious tide.

When the fire is finally roaring—the heat warming me—I kick off my shoes and curl my toes into the damp bed of grass beneath my feet. Earth's slimy carpet feels good and spongy as if it were a springboard from which I could leap at any moment.

I suddenly feel weightless, as if all the contents of my body had been drawn out in a single breath. The string tethering me to the ground snaps like a fishing line and I sense my feet lifting, my body slowly rising into the air.

I feel free. I don't belong to anyone. And nobody belongs to me.

Not Grace.

Not Maud.

Not Mia.

Not even the scrap of paper with Charlotte's name scrawled

across it.

I find myself with arms outstretched, my body sailing toward the open mouth of the inferno as if I were being beckoned by the ghost of a long lost loved one.

I meet them and am greeted by a warm embrace, flames wrapping around me with loving fingers made of smoke.

I'm pulled deeper into their arms, petals of fire weaving through my hair, until I'm gently rocked to sleep the same way a mother swaddles a child.

THE STRANGE THING WE BECOME

title/a human stain
thread/thestrangethingwebecome
Posted by mummyqueerest 409 days ago
[78 comments] <u>Click here</u> to share with your followers

TRYING THIS OUT. JUST TO see how it goes. I'm not really sure where to start.

We just got back from a four-hour drive from the doctor. Mass General. A cement truck flipped over and sideswiped a Mazda on I-95 North. All lanes stopped. Gridlock. Nobody hurt, thankfully.

Maybe it's because I'm jet lagged from the red-eye I took into Boston or because I'm still hungover from my "Welcome Home" dinner last night, but I keep imagining I smell a very particular scent.

Makes me think of my father.

I remember him telling me how when a whitetail fawn is born, it's born without a smell.

He had said that their scent glands are so undeveloped that

22

they hardly give off any odor at all.

It's like they're invisible.

That's nature's design of camouflaging something so helpless from becoming prey. To keep track of her offspring, the doe will lick her fawn and wash it with her scent. Never bedding in the same place for too long, the mother will migrate through the woods to keep her baby from predators.

But, as they keep moving from nest to nest, the mother has to keep marking the fawn with her scent. It's not long before the fawn inherits its mother's odor until it becomes a rich smell of its own.

That's when it becomes perfumed prey.

My father often told me that humans are not so dissimilar. Because no matter how perfect we are when we're born, in this world we can't stay clean forever.

I often think of why he told me that when I was so young.

I wonder if the thought upset him when he had to take care of my mother before she died. Perhaps he had imagined her guttural wet cough staining his face with permanent ash visible only to him. Maybe she had touched him gently and he had sensed her leave behind unseen glistening black oily threads from where her hands had been.

I remember how he washed himself more regularly after we had buried her. Scrubbing forcefully. Not with meticulousness. But with visible dread.

I wonder if it's because each thing that loves us leaves behind a small stain.

title/fuck cancer
thread/thestrangethingwebecome
Posted by mummyqueerest 386 days ago
[106 comments] <u>Click here</u> to share with your followers

I've only felt truly hurt three times in my life.

Once was when I was six years old and one of the kids in our neighborhood called me a "monster." It was because I preferred to cut my hair shorter than the other girls and because I wore shirts two sizes too big to cover the breasts I didn't want. I spent so many years hiding from mirrors as if I were going to be greeted by the very thing he had shouted at me. Imagine my surprise when someone as beautiful as Evie actually wanted me.

More importantly, someone who wanted to have children with me.

She would wrap her arms around my shoulders and pant in my ear— "our first born will be named Emil. After your father." I would laugh to hide nervousness and promise her it was a deal as long as our next adopted child would be named after her mother, Rosemary. I never cared too much about the names. Or even children, for that matter. Children have never liked me, and I've never really liked them. I just wanted a baby because I knew it would make her happy.

The second time I felt hurt was after my mother started chemotherapy and I watched her comb clumps of hair as thick as hay from her liver-spot-dotted head. Once she was left with nothing but a glowing halo, one of the neighbor's kids made fun of my father and said he had married a man. They said I must've caught my queerness from him. It's funny how other people know things about you before you know them.

The only other time I've felt truly hurt was yesterday afternoon when Evie and I were sitting in a waiting room at Mass General after Dr. Pierson delivered us the news. She took both of my hands. Her eyes—wet and shining—begged me a soundless question. Breath whistling, she finally said, "what about Emil?"

Dr. Pierson later answered her in the exam room with the word: "Terminal."

I watched Evie shrink, a balloon emptying of all air. Hands falling at her side, her palms facing outward with mother-like attendance began to close like crocuses after sunset.

I think her reaction to the news wounded me so much because it made me realize she didn't care what might happen to her. Evie was far more concerned about the child we could no longer afford to adopt because of medical bills. Now, a funeral, too.

I wish I could have given her a child.

I've given her nothing.

She deserved so much more than to be loved by a monster like me.

title/death is a dark room without a door

THE STRANGE THING WE BECOME

thread/thestrangethingwebecome
Posted by mummyqueerest 369 days ago
[89 comments] <u>Click here</u> to share with your followers

Thank you so much for all of the kind and thoughtful comments on my previous post. I read each one to Evie last night during dinner.

I promise this thread won't be entirely depressing bullshit. I can't make that promise for this post, but bear with me in the meantime.

Today was a better day. Thankfully.

Evie has been an angel. I was careful to keep my hands steady as I washed the dirty plates after dinner or else she would've devoted an hour trying to console me again. Whenever she sees my eyes glisten or my lips start to quiver, she takes my hands in hers and blows her breath against my face. As if just letting me know she's still here. I feel silly relying on little moments like these, but she says it's payback for all the nights I stayed awake with her.

Evie never liked going to sleep because of what happened to her when she was in elementary school. I asked for her permission to tell the story, and she said it would be OK since this—whatever this online forum is—has been such a healthy part of the coping process. It's brought Evie and I even closer. So, silver linings. Right?

When Evie was seven, her mother and father separated, and her mother was awarded full custody. Evie's words are few when it comes to describing her father. A red, angry-looking face, an easily frowning mouth—those aren't her words; they're mine from the few pictures of him I've seen. A butcher with a well-known temper at the local market, the stench of raw meat shadowed him constantly, and Evie told me she had to plug her nose whenever he came near at bedtime.

She smelled his familiar scent one morning on the playground. He was loitering on the other side of the fence, a can of cherry coke in his hand and a cigarette hanging from his lip. Dangling a brand-new coloring book in front of her the way a fisherman might lure a small fish, she went to him with little hesitation, and it wasn't long before she was sliding into the backseat of his Oldsmobile.

It was the day in March the temperature got to over a hundred degrees. We were kids then, but our parents remember it. They remember reading about the little girl who almost died after her father left her in the car with the windows rolled up while he went to the nearest bar. What they didn't read about in the papers was that Evie was pronounced dead at the hospital for twelve seconds.

I've only asked her about it once—what she saw, what it was like.

She looked at me, troubled. As if she had been dreading my curiosity.

"Nothing," she said. "It's like nothing."

title/whistle and i'll come
thread/thestrangethingwebecome
Posted by mummyqueerest 344 days ago
[43 comments] Click here to share with your followers

Evie's stopped checking the forum, so she jokes I can post whatever I want on here now.

Didn't get much sleep last night. Helped Evie clean the bathroom after she had gotten sick. It's agonizing to watch her symptoms become more like habits with each passing day. She used to sob whenever she would throw up—hands covering her mouth, eyes wet and sparkling. Now, I watch her amble to the toilet and lean her head over the bowl without comment as if she were performing the same ritual a janitor might when they empty a bucket and mop.

Does anyone have any suggestions for food that won't upset her stomach so much? We've stocked up on chicken, eggs, beans, and nuts. But maybe I'm missing something?

I've found her in the attic lately. Legs folded. Eyes closed. Arms at her side. Sometimes she doesn't even hear me when I walk in. I'll say something and it's as if she's lost somewhere behind her eyelids—buried deep in some secret part of herself. I whistle at her, wooing her to come back to Earth and like a dozing toddler she always returns.

I ask her what she thinks about when she's there.

The answer is always the same. "Nothing."

THE STRANGE THING WE BECOME

title/angel on fire
thread/thestrangethingwebecome
Posted by mummyqueerest 221 days ago
[134 comments] <u>Click here</u> to share with your followers

Did you ever hear of Nadezhda Konopka?

Probably not.

Back in the 1970's, Bulgarian performance art wasn't necessarily newsworthy even if she's considered one of the most despised provocateurs of the twentieth century. I'm sure you're googling her name right now, but I'll tell you about some of her notable exhibitions:

1. Had her clitoris removed during a public circumcision ritual to bring attention to the horrors of female genital mutilation in Sudan.

2. Had her left arm removed completely in a public performance dedicated to deforestation and climate change.

3. Was force fed horse shit for seven hours in an act of resistance against the current political administration.

Those were some of her more conservative performances. I'll spare you the details of some of her more disgusting exhibitions. Regardless, she made Marina Abramovic look like Mother Teresa. She's probably not as well-known because those around her claimed she had the personality of a stuffed animal wrapped in barbed wire.

Anyway, Evie's obsessed with her. Especially one of her performances in particular. Her final one— "Angel on Fire." Nadezhda didn't live very long; nobody knew exactly how old she was when she died, but they speculated mid- to late forties. The way she chose to end her life was especially mystifying. In a year-long event held in Belgrade, Nadezhda committed to the act of self-mummification.

You're probably opening another tab and googling right now, right? I had never heard of it either until I read through the links saved on Evie's phone. A ritual based in Buddhism, monks would often attempt this gruesome ritual in order to transcend death and achieve the ultimate enlightenment.

After months of self-deprivation, she was placed in a tomb with a small bell she would ring daily in order to signal she was still alive. Finally the day arrived when the bell didn't ring and her tomb was sealed. After a year had passed, they opened the tomb and discovered she had indeed successfully preserved herself like the ancient monks.

Her body was removed from the tomb and placed in a bulletproof glass case in a small square in her hometown of Shumata. She's still there on display to this very day. I think in the mid-90s a group of high schoolers tried to blow up the shrine with makeshift explosives but were stopped before they could do any serious damage.

Evie's wanted to visit her shrine for years now. I didn't have the heart to tell her, but before the diagnosis I had booked us two tickets to Bulgaria for Christmas this year. I wanted to surprise her, but the doctor says she can't travel.

Then, of course, there's the horrible thought I can't seem to push out from my mind—will she be around for Christmas?

title/something bad
thread/thestrangethingwebecome
Posted by mummyqueerest 295 days ago
[95 comments] Click here to share with your followers

I did something bad.

There. I said it.

Well, typed it.

That's half the battle, right? Admitting to yourself you did something horrible.

Some people do terrible things and never put words to what they've done. But at least I'm acknowledging the fact that I fucked up. It may not make me a better person than the people who do horrible things. But it has to count for something. Right?

I've written out this post twelve times now. Deleted it every time. I'm not going to rewrite it for a thirteenth. I'm just going to tell you what happened.

Evie's spending most of her time in the attic, meditating. I've asked if I can come in—sit with her and read—but she doesn't want to be distracted.

She's been seeming so much more distant lately. She doesn't even open her eyes when I whistle. I can't tell if it's because she's too far gone or simply because she just doesn't want to.

We hardly talk anymore. Sometimes we go the entire day without speaking unless I make an attempt at conversation.

I was rummaging through the boxes in the attic and came across my grandfather's Morse code machine. He taught me how to use it during the summer I spent at his lake house when I turned eleven. Never thought it would still work. I started tinkering with it again out of boredom, trying to re-familiarize myself with the different letters he had taught me.

Dot-dash for the letter A. *Dash-dot-dot-dot* for the letter B. *Dash-dot-dash-dot* for C. I won't bore you with the whole alphabet. You get the picture.

The thing I love most about Morse code is that it slows you down. It makes you consider the shape of each letter; makes you mindful of the meaning behind every word. I used to spend hours in the basement typing out messages to the ghosts I imagined haunting my grandfather's lake house. Sometimes I'd pretend I was writing my diary and would write each entry in the third person— "She saw a robin today" or "her grandfather bought her new patent leather shoes for her birthday."

Although I didn't expect Evie to share my excitement for locating my grandfather's Morse code machine, I hardly expected her to remain so cold and unfeeling. I presented it to her, trying to coax even just one word from her lips stretched thin like elastic bands.

"Isn't this something?" I teased. Not my most beguiling conversation starter, but I wanted some sort of reaction from her—anything. Instead she merely sat there—eyes closed, legs folded, hands tucked in her lap. Testing her comfort, the way a small child might approach an animal, I drew closer and searched her body for a sign of acknowledgement. I saw her ears pin the way a horse's do as I stepped closer, the floorboards creaking beneath my weight. She wasn't sleeping. Wasn't even meditating. She was pretending I wasn't there.

I got the message. So, I figured I'd send her one, too.

I took the Morse code machine, and I started tapping.

Fuck-*dash*-you-*dash*-fucking-*dash*-bitch.

The machine chirped like a furious sparrow, my finger springing up and down as if it were hammering each letter into her skull. Tap, tap, tap. An invisible blade chiseling away the silence she had put between us.

I'm-*dash*-not-*dash*-going-*dash*-to-*dash*-even-*dash*-miss-*dash*-you-*dash*-when-

dash-you're-*dash*-fucking-*dash*-gone.

I imagined every word spraying her as if they were darts, each dash a needle-thin tip gluing to her skin. How could she treat me like this? To be so cruel even when she knows our time is precious.

When I was finished, I didn't feel any better. I felt worse when I watched her open her eyes.

It was the way she looked at me.

It was as if she understood.

title/if elephants can remember, let me forget
thread/thestrangethingwebecome
Posted by mummyqueerest 276 days ago
[67 comments] Click here to share with your followers

She's not the same person she once was.

There are times when I look at her and I struggle to recognize the woman I once fell in love with, desperately searching for her and hoping she's buried somewhere beneath what I see. It's as if she's blurred behind a rain-soaked window that I can't open. That must be what it's like to look at the face of God.

I once read somewhere that most elephants don't die of old age. Instead, their teeth become brittle and break off, forcing them to starve to death. I always wondered if they knew exactly what was happening to them; if they were somehow very much aware of their suffering; if they knew they were completely helpless to what they had become.

Since they have the sharpest memories in the animal kingdom, I wonder how excruciating it must be for them to recognize themselves changing and being at the mercy of inevitability. I suppose all living things are. Humans are just able to put words to it. We've invented euphemisms to dull the way an affliction sounds, but not necessarily how it feels. I think that's the most dangerous part about being human—conceiving nice ways of saying something truly terrible.

The doctors told me Evie would change. Cancer does that to a person. It empties them out until they're as barren as a locust-eaten field of grain. What the doctors didn't tell me was how much I would change while watching her suffer. I shouldn't be so surprised though. Each thing we love takes a little piece of us whether we give it willingly or not. By the time we find the person we were meant to be with, we're a honeycombed shell of what we once were. Each person we love turns us into the strange thing we become.

That's why I decided to call this thread "The Strange Thing We Become." It's also the title of the book I'm writing about Evie and her battle with cancer. I wouldn't be able to do any of this without your kind messages. I've been thinking lately about the person I was before I had met her—how different I was.

But sometimes I wish we could forget who we were before we loved and lost someone.

I wonder if we'd be happier.

Evie's been happy lately. Changed her phone passcode, which I thought was strange. She doesn't meditate as much. Instead, she's been exercising and losing so much weight. It's starting to scare me. She's glued herself to the elliptical—arms and legs pumping when I leave in the morning and still working when I return late at night from work. She's been eating bizarre things, too—only buckwheat, millets, or raw vegetables. Nothing else.

One of the strangest things happened the other night. She's been drinking this horrible-smelling imported tea she said the doctor said would help her immune system. But it fucks with her stomach like nothing else. I found her huddled in the attic, sitting in a pile of her own excrement. She was so lost in her meditation she didn't even realize she had soiled herself. When I woke her, she didn't believe me until I started cleaning the filth sliming the backs of her legs.

I don't even cry anymore when I clean up her sick or wipe the filth from her. Maybe I'm not the same person I once was either.

title/three words
thread/thestrangethingwebecome
Posted by mummyqueerest 254 days ago
[47 comments] <u>Click here</u> to share with your followers

I never thought I'd have to write something like this. I've been going over the words in my mind again and again. I can't seem to make sense of any of it. Everything leads me back to the same place—the same thought. No matter how horrible it is.

I think Evie's having an affair.

I came home late from work last night, hoping to surprise her with takeout. I found her in her usual place— crouching on the attic floor with head lowered and eyes closed like a prisoner awaiting execution. I thought to wake her, but I noticed something lying beside her on the floor—a silver wedding band.

Not hers.

I rushed to the bathroom because I thought I was going to be sick, and I found the shower nozzle had been adjusted, the faucet gently dripping. The fresh smell of aftershave burned the hairs in my nose. It was as if they weren't even trying to hide themselves—such eagerness to be caught.

I returned to the attic and sat down across from her, waiting for her to open her eyes. I knew if I wanted an answer, I'd go wanting. I placed the Morse code machine between us and started tapping.

How-*dash*-could-*dash*-you-*dash*-do-*dash*-this-*dash*-to-*dash*-me-*dash*-after-*dash*-

all-*dash*-I've-*dash*-done-*dash*-for-*dash*-you?

I waited for a moment, imagining each dash forming a long rope and lassoing itself around her neck. Squeezing tight, I'd pull the answer from the pit of her fear-clogged throat.

Her hands answered first, long skeletal fingers pressing down on the key and slowly tapping.

When she was finished, the three words she had spelled hung in the air like a dim vapor only I could see:

I-*dash*-love-*dash*-you.

title/something's wrong
thread/thestrangethingwebecome
Posted by mummyqueerest 189 days ago
[61 comments] <u>Click here</u> to share with your followers

She's getting way too thin. Hardly ever eats. Her arms—like toothpicks. Her skin—fever-yellow and as transparent as wax paper. Found out she missed her last two doctor appointments after she lied and told me one of our neighbors had driven her there.

I'm wondering if I should take her to the hospital.

THE STRANGE THING WE BECOME

Thank you for your messages. Please keep us in your thoughts.

title/help
thread/thestrangethingwebecome
Posted by mummyqueerest 102 days ago
[59 comments] <u>Click here</u> to share with your followers

I don't know if I can even write it out. It hurts too much.
God, I feel sick. I think I'm going to throw up.

title/no room for poetry
thread/thestrangethingwebecome
Posted by mummyqueerest 102 days ago
[109 comments] <u>Click here</u> to share with your followers

There's no room for poetry here.
She's pregnant.

title/the red carrot in the shoebox
thread/thestrangethingwebecome
Posted by mummyqueerest 83 days ago
[52 comments] <u>Click here</u> to share with your followers

Did you hear the one about the woman who worked at the shoe store?
She puffed up. Get it? The woman at the shoe store puffed up. Big.
But, when she finally deflated, she was sad because she had to put a tiny carrot inside a shoebox and carry it with her wherever she went. The carrot was wet and red, impossibly small. You could hold it in the palm of your hand if you tried.
She tried. Pushed and pushed. Waiting to hear tiny screams that never came.
There's no punchline to the story. Just a small red carrot dressed in overalls two sizes too big.
I always hated that story.

title/our baby boy
thread/thestrangethingwebecome

Posted by mummyqueerest 75 days ago
[37 comments] Click here to share with your followers

Went to check on Evie this morning and found the red carrot from the story between her legs on the floor. I'm holding it in my arms as I'm typing this.
No. Not "it."
Him.
His name is Emil.

title/in the dark room
thread/thestrangethingwebecome
Posted by mummyqueerest 54 days ago
[94 comments] Click here to share with your followers

I have nothing left to live for.

title/this angel burns too
thread/thestrangethingwebecome
Posted by mummyqueerest 9 days ago
[159 comments] Click here to share with your followers

If you're reading this, Evie's dead.
I feel cold air pass through me, a small invisible hand raking through my insides as if it were searching for something it can't find. The hole I opened in my abdomen must've been a deep one. I quietly thank God for little mercies such as that. It'll be over soon.
I tucked Evie's hands in her lap, cleaned the wetness from between her legs. She almost resembles Nadezhda in her little tomb—legs folded, shoulders buckled like a loosened marionette doll, head lowered as if in prayer.
It won't be long until we're all together again.
Until then, I'll wander the house—whistling, carrying the small red carrot—like an elephant that forgot it's starving.

THE TREES GREW BECAUSE I BLED THERE

"I HAVE BAD NEWS," I tell him, an admonition I know he won't hear.

It's the very least I can do; to warn him.

Instead, he's far too preoccupied inspecting the artistry of his cravat or reviewing the craftsmanship of his diamond wristwatch I had given him two years ago—little souvenirs I had thought might tide him over before he had expected more gruesomely intimate offerings.

"Where were you?" he asks, occasionally glancing up at me.

I wheel myself further into the room, almost expecting him to recoil in horror at the crude patchwork of human anatomy he's made of me—the bandage covering the hollow socket where my right eye has been shoveled out, and the cloth wrapped around the blistered nubs where my feet once were.

I'm an insult to his beauty, an offense to his handsomeness and charm.

"I went to the park to water the trees," I tell him. "They were thirsty today."

I notice the glass of water I had left for him on the table and suddenly wonder if the unpleasantness of my task has already been done.

"Did you drink anything?"

"Am I not allowed?" he asks me.

I'm already wheeling myself toward the apartment's kitchenette, preparing to pour him a drink from the pitcher I had arranged on the counter. "Let me get you something."

"You're late," he says.

Without warning, he's reduced me to the size of a dressmaker's thimble, my stomach curling at his obvious disappointment. It's the very same defeat I had once felt when I had frustrated my father. I straighten in my now permanent chair, as if suddenly remembering I'm no longer a child, no longer a servant to the capricious whims of a taskmaster.

"I have bad news," I say again.

"You said you'd be here—" he says, referring to his wristwatch and ignoring me.

"Really bad news," I repeat.

"—twenty-four minutes ago."

"Exceptionally horrible bad news."

"Incidentally the same number of teeth you still owe me," he says, stretching open his lips and tapping his front teeth with his index finger. "Twenty-four."

"The kind of news that might make you prefer to be flayed alive and then dipped head-first into a vat of boiling hot wax," I say.

His face seems to soften slightly, the color in his cheeks draining as if poisoned by the dangerous thought. "I was worried you wouldn't show."

But I'm far too excited to be contained now. "Or to have your skull smashed open by a mallet and then your brain scrambled with an ice pick."

He looks at me suddenly with a wordless threat. "Where is it?"

"That's all you care about," I say, deflating and turning away from him.

He scurries after me the way an insect stalks its prey, promising me it's not true. When the room is quiet again—so quiet I can imagine I can hear the blood pulsing and pooling inside him—he approaches me as if he were nearing a small animal caught in a steel-trap.

"What kept you?" he asks me.

The center of my chest throbs with a dull ache, the place where my heart once was now nothing more than a desecrated bed of flowers—stems slashed, roots plucked and torn out.

"Took longer than expected," I say, agony stretching its little fingers to the most private and unspoiled parts inside me. "I told you it gets harder every time."

He marvels at me with the same wide, hopeful eyes of a schoolboy observing an older woman undress.

"I've always wanted to watch," he says.

I remove the red Chinese paper lantern from the lamp beside the bed, as if it were a signal to him that we won't be making love tonight. If you could even call it "making love," that is. Our moments of intimacy, few and far between, were about as delicate as a mortician with a fresh cadaver.

"I only do it when I'm alone," I remind him.

He asks me why.

"Works better that way."

"Doesn't hurt?" he asks me, as if suddenly pretending to care.

"Anything that's worth doing always hurts," I tell him.

He's persistent, shadowing me as I wheel myself around the room and scoop armfuls of dirty clothing littered about the floor.

"Show me," he begs.

I notice the corners of my lips creasing in what I think is a smile. I enjoy watching him beg. "Wouldn't mean as much to you if I showed you," I tell him, as if quietly hopeful he'll resort to more tender means to convince me.

"Still would."

I toss a handful of dirty clothes into the hamper, folding my arms when I turn to him. "Christmas isn't the same when you realize the only thing at the North Pole is a giant hole in the ozone."

"That doesn't stop people from wanting presents," he says. "Speaking of. You have something for me?"

I suddenly remember the small pine box I had arranged in my lap—my precious gift to him. I scoop it up in my hands, my fingers going over each of the box's corners.

"You've been waiting for this one for a while, haven't you?" I ask him.

He merely nods.

"How long?"

He clears the catch in his throat, quietly rehearsing his answer. "Since you first gave me your eye."

The one remaining blinks. "I gave it because I knew you'd take care of it."

For once, he appears delicate, fragile, as if he were incapable of hurting anything. "Kept it from drying out. Propped it on a little velvet pillow," he says, far away and distant.

I humor him, laughing. "What did you name it?"

"How could you forget, Lovely?" he asks, teasing me.

My laugh shrinks until it's a pitiful whisper when I'm reminded of why I'm here. I feel myself tighten as if my every extremity were filling with cement. "Too busy thinking about the bad news I have to tell you."

He suddenly pales, as if realizing and suddenly imagining the worst. "You don't have it."

"That's not it," I say, shaking my head.

He lunges for me, swiping at the pine box. But I'm too quick for him, pulling away and guarding the precious gift with both hands.

He's on me again in a matter of seconds. "I want to see it."

"You're not going to like what I have to tell you," I warn him. The words are my only defense.

He retreats slightly, arms lowering to his sides. "I'm listening."

The words don't come easy at first. They come to me in little fragments—a puzzle I cannot solve.

"I thought about keeping something," I blurt out. "For myself. There. I said it. Removing another part of me, but not telling you about it."

I search him for a semblance of emotion. "Are you mad?"

He looks at me, incredulous. "Am I mad?"

I tell him how I had wondered what I could keep without him noticing. One of my teeth? No, I knew he would count them. A fingernail, maybe. He'd count them, too. Then, I tell him how it came to me: I walk around covered in something that always grow back no matter how much you remove—skin.

I explain how I took a knife and cut the back of my leg because it was fat and muscly. I tell him how I felt blood—warm and sticky like the syrup from a maple tree—trickle from the small hole I had opened along my calf. I explain how I had carved out a piece of my skin and pinched it between my fingers as it wiggled there, wet and oily like a salamander's tail.

Then, I tell him how I threw a pan on the stove and turned up the gas. I explain how I dropped some butter in the pan and watched my piece of skin skate around the edges until it started to crackle and crisp like a strip of bacon. I tell him how when the edges started to brown, I skewered it with a fork and swallowed it whole. It was like chewing on cooked rubber. But it tasted exquisite.

"Do you know why?" I ask him. "It was something I could keep for myself. Something I couldn't give away. Something I could keep for me."

I wait for him to say something. He merely lowers his head.

"You said you'd give me your skin when we were done," he says to me with all the petulance of a spurned toddler.

I feel myself threatening to come apart, the little bits that remain of me untethering and beginning to float away. "I know."

"You broke the rules," he says, turning and folding his arms. "You said you'd give me everything. No matter how painful."

"And I have," I say, wheeling myself after him and pleading. "I promise. I just . . . I wanted to keep something—for me. I dream about giving you all I have. You know that."

"I don't know what you dream about."

I go to reach for him and for a moment our hands touch. I had forgotten how creamy and smooth his skin was.

"Let's tell each other," I beg him.

He recoils, pushing me away. "You don't want to know."

Perhaps this is my chance to stop something terrible from happening. Perhaps I don't have to go through with it.

"How long have you known me?" I ask him.

He hesitates. "Two years."

The center of my chest aches again—where my heart used to be. How could he not remember it's been three years? He pales when I remind him.

"Has it—?" he asks me, recoiling like a mouse from a trap.

My voice is thin, hollow. "Three this summer."

His eyes search me for an explanation, almost as if he were scouring me for a reason to stay. "Yes."

"You know I keep nothing from you," I say. "Why can't you

do the same for me?"

He lowers his head, the light reflecting from his eyes starting to dim as if the pitiful flame smoldering inside him were finally being snuffed out.

"Last night I dreamt I was a baby again," he tells me. "My cradle was a giant cutting board. My arms and legs were fat like tubes of sausages. My head was the size of a watermelon that God had made just so He could use a hammer to split wide open. And He did."

He tells me how he spilled out and little pieces of him crept across the board like a leaking egg yolk. He says as he wiggled there, he realized he could speak. So, he asked God, "Why?"

"That's the question everyone would ask, right?" he says. "Not 'What happens after we die?' Or 'How do we cure cancer?' The one thing everyone would ask if they met God is 'Why did you do this to me?' And do you know what He said? He tilted his fork at me and said, 'We're going to start with you again.'"

He shudders, doubling over and guarding his stomach, as if his intestines were being poked and prodded by an invisible deity.

"So, He mashed me up into little bite sized pieces and stuffed me into His mouth," he says. "I think that's what happens to us after we die. God gobbles us up and then shits us out as someone—something—new."

He stares at me, as if hopeful I'll say something. For once, I'm not tethered to his words as if they were the only thing from keeping my anatomy from coming apart. In fact, I find myself indulging in his discomfort as he stirs, surrounded by quiet. There's something so inviting about observing his uneasiness— an unsure visitor in a predator's empty mountain den.

"What do you think you'd come back as?" he asks me.

I think for a moment, savoring his distress. After all, I know it's going to get much worse.

"I'd like to be a tree," I say. "A Rosewood Tree that leaks sap as red and as thick as blood when you cut it."

I imagine my arms hardening into branches, my hair exploding with tiny emerald buds until I'm a beloved secret tucked away in some distant field—a birthplace for small birds and insects, a hallowed sanctuary for the weak and the afflicted.

"Why?" he asks me.

"Because you can cut their branches off and they heal," I tell him. "Then, tiny buds bloom and little branches sprout in new places. I could give you as much of me as I possibly could. I could carve out an eye and then grow a new one. People wouldn't stare as much. I wouldn't get looked at in the streets."

"You always said you didn't care."

"Lately I do."

His voice thins to a whisper as he approaches me, his head lowered. "I have bad news, too," he says.

I simper quietly, taking comfort in the fact that his news certainly can't be worse than mine.

"The kind of news that'll make me want to wrap my hair in tin foil and stick my head inside a microwave?" I ask, as if daring him.

"She and I are going to be married," he says. "Next month."

It's then I notice the small wedding band on his finger, the silver glinting in the light. My grip on the pine box weakens, my whole body seeming to loosen.

"I . . . thought you said it was off," I say.

"I did. It was. But things . . . change. That's why I can't stay long. She's—"

"Waiting for you," I say, finishing his sentence.

He nods. Then, he begins to undress. First, he unbuttons his shirt, revealing a physique worthy of a Grecian athlete. Then, he unzips and slides his pants down until they're crumpled around his ankles.

"I thought that's why you wanted to meet here at my place," I say.

He wrenches the silver wedding band from his finger and places it on the kitchen counter. "This might be the last time for a while."

"For a while?"

"At least until I can figure out how I can see you again," he says.

I can't hurt him. Not yet. "What about everything I've given you?"

"She thinks you're crazy—"

He stops, inhaling sharply when he realizes. He flashes me a wordless apology with the slightest look.

"I mean, she's . . . surprised . . . you've given so much to me," he says. "She doesn't usually—She doesn't like when I ask for things. I'm lucky to collect a few strands of hair. A few eyelashes. But my prized possession is one of her fingers."

I sense myself crumpling like discarded trash, as if I were nothing more than a hairbrush filled with lice, or a white bedsheet stained with menstrual blood.

"She's . . . given you things, too?" I ask, avoiding even looking at him.

"Only the few times I've asked her."

"You said I was the only one," I say, my voice breaking apart as if my throat were filled with stones. "I . . . thought I was the only one who gave you . . . I gave you those pieces to protect. I gave you them because you said you loved me. Still love me."

"I do," he says. "Did, I mean. I told you. Things have changed. Like a tree changes when it regrows one of its branches. It grows different. Misshapen. Malformed. Isn't that how you've . . ."

Once again, he stops himself as his cheeks redden.

"Isn't that how we've become?" he says.

Finally. The moment I've been waiting for. He reaches for the glass of water on the table and presses his lips against the rim of the glass. He takes a long, steady drink. I watch him silently as he gulps it down.

Perhaps it's time I tell him.

"I still have to tell you the really bad news," I say.

"Should I sit down for this?" he asks.

"Won't make a difference."

He looks at me bewildered, eyes searching me for an answer. I extend my hand, passing the small pine box to him. He takes it and opens it. His face scrunches slightly, flipping the box upside down and shaking it.

"It's empty?"

There's no pleasure to be found in his puzzlement. This hurts me more than he'll ever know. "I have to fill it with things," I tell him.

It's then that he begins to cough. He doubles over, coughing until hoarse into his fist.

"Fill it with what?" he asks me, his eyes wet and shining.

I'm circling him the way a leopard corners an infant animal separated from its mother.

"Things only you can give me," I tell him.

It's not before long he's bent down on his knees, covering his mouth as he coughs violently.

"Where is it?" he demands to know.

"I'm keeping it in a special place for now. You see, you're not just hurting me anymore when you take something. There's someone else you're hurting, too."

His lips crinkle, eyebrows furrowed as he glares at me. A momentary respite from the coughing. "Someone else?"

I answer him without words, merely glancing down and rubbing my stomach—the precious life I've been carrying for three weeks now.

His eyes widen, understanding.

"You mean you're—?"

He can't even say the word.

I nod.

He wipes threads of spit from his mouth, clearing his throat. "I thought you couldn't . . . We always used a—"

"Did we?" I ask him.

He pauses for a moment, as if surprised by my sudden brashness.

I wheel myself into the kitchenette, preparing for the unpleasantness of the task at hand. This could have all been avoided if we had never made love; if we had never come to such a dreadful arrangement where one person gives and the other merely takes and takes.

He crawls after me on hands and knees, coughing violently.

"You want money? Is that it?"

I'm at the pantry, rummaging through the shelves before I finally recover what I'm looking for—a large picnic blanket. I unfurl the checkered blanket and spread it out until it's completely covering the kitchenette's tiled floor.

"I don't need money," I tell him.

"I'll give you money," he says, chasing after me and spasming in agony. "If that'll keep you quiet. Keep you away. Just tell me how much you want."

"It's not what I want," I tell him. "It's what our child wants. What our baby needs. A child needs their father's love. Their father's heart."

He collapses to the ground with a vulgar thud, splayed out on the checkered picnic blanket. His chest slowly rises and falls. He's

43

still alive, and I quietly thank God for that.

"I . . . can't move," he whimpers.

"You will again when I'm finished," I assure him, dragging a knife from the kitchen counter and brandishing it. "You're going to give our child everything I've given you and more. He'll have your eyes. Your fingers. Your toes. Every piece of you I can take. That way, when you're not around, he'll know how much his father loved him. No matter what."

He whimpers, squirming on the ground as if he had been lassoed like livestock. For once, I feel pity for him as I watch him twitch there helplessly like a small animal caught in the throes of a grand mal seizure.

I steel my resolve, remembering the precious life I carry inside me, as I grip the knife's handle. Crawling out of my chair, I push myself against him and swaddle him like a mother dismissing a child's nightmare with a mere embrace. I wrap my arms around him as he twitches and cradle him until he's finally without movement, his suffering eased for the moment.

He dozes, probably dreaming of bicycling down a woodland path or sprinting across a deserted field—things he'll never be able to do again after I've finished my work.

I prepare the knife, and as I marvel at him, I can't help but wish he were like a tree.

YOU'RE NOT SUPPOSED TO BE HERE

"YOU'RE NOT SUPPOSED TO BE here," he says to us with such matter-of-fact ease that it almost sounds reassuring.

The way he says it doesn't frighten me the way it should.

Or perhaps even the way it was intended to.

It's the tender voice of a shepherd; a gentle caregiver steering an elderly patient toward their deathbed.

It's the delicate voice of a schoolteacher; an instructor coming to the rescue of a frightened child.

His voice is convincing and firm, as if he knows where we belong instead and he's the only herdsman capable of guiding us there. It sounds as if it were an invitation as opposed to a refusal—an opportunity to finally belong somewhere and belong in such a way that our presence will never be questioned by another ever again. It sounds as if he knows something that we don't, an eagerness pinched in the pit of his throat and frantic to reveal his secrets.

I'll never forget the way he had first approached us—the confidence in his stride as he steered across the emerald lawn, weaving in between the small children playing croquet with their parents. It had seemed as though he were immediately drawn to us, like a bumble bee to a bush of lilac. His eyes—shining like discarded beads left in sunlight—had narrowed at me, not with a question, but with an answer for which I didn't recall asking.

I've always been of the unsuspecting sort and prone to admitting defeat even when I was in the right. My husband had always said that if I were a flower, my stem would bend even if there wasn't any wind.

As the man in the checkered blue shirt tilts his horn-rimmed eyeglasses at us, my husband stops me before I have the opportunity to blurt out a senseless apology.

"Not supposed to be where?" he asks, raising a hand to cover his eyes until the stranger steps in front of the summer sun glaring down at us like the bleached white bone of a prehistoric monster.

Our six-month-old baby named Philip stirs on the blanket we've set out on the ground for him. His freckled face creases with a smile, his auburn curls shimmering in the sunlight. He fiddles with one of the silver buttons decorating his plaid overalls, screeching with glee as if he were also questioning the strange man.

"Here," the man says, his voice hardening as if we should know full well what he's talking about. His silhouette flickers against the tree like the seared outline of a human body vaporized in a nuclear explosion. He repeats it once more: "You're not supposed to be here."

Vince's eyes dart to me for a moment, as if incredulous. He draws in a labored breath, obviously preparing for the worst, as he pushes himself off both knees and rises to his feet. Steadying himself like a toddler who's just learned how to walk, he's shorter than the man in the checkered shirt by at least several inches.

Vince seems to immediately recognize this embarrassment as he shrinks slightly at the realization, his hands closing to fists like tulips at nighttime. I watch him as he stiffens the way a small animal inflates to fend off larger nocturnal predators, his shoulders widening and his spine straightening.

"I'm sorry," he says. Finally, an apology. "Did we take your spot?"

The man, bewildered, looks at me as if he expects me to understand. His eyes linger long enough to make me feel awkward, so I merely shake my head, shrugging. The man's eyes return to Vince, the corners of his mouth creasing in what appears to be the beginnings of a smile.

"That phrase doesn't mean anything to you?" he asks, resting both of his hands on his hips and revealing dark stains blossoming from beneath both of his arms.

"No," Vince says, folding his arms as if it were his last defense. "Should it?"

"You're not Craig Baker?" the man asks.

Vince glances at me, his glare softening at the realization of the mistake.

Finally. An explanation for the man's unusual behavior.

"I'm not," Vince says, shaking his head and face thawing with a polite smile as if saddened to disappoint him.

"You must think I'm a lunatic," the man says, warmth pooling in both his cheeks. "I'm so sorry to bother you. I thought you were my pen pal."

The word initially jars me—pen pal. I sense myself tightening, thinking to myself, *What grown man has a pen pal? Or, at the very least, admits to the fact?*

The man extends his right hand for Vince to shake and reveals his entire hand has been bandaged with cloth. Fingers as thick as tubes of blood sausages poke through some of the dressings. Some of the bandages have been rusted brown with dried blood.

Vince goes to shake his hand but stops halfway when he realizes. The man, obviously already embarrassed, snaps his hand back as if silently cursing his forgetfulness.

"I'm sorry," he says, shoving his bandaged hand underneath his armpit. "It's new."

The man resumes, offering his left hand.

"I'm Lyric," he says. "Easy to remember. A beautiful melody is nothing without a—"

"Lyric," Vince finishes, shaking his hand.

He laughs slightly. It's a laugh I can't help but recognize too well.

It's the same laugh I'm acquainted with when we're out to dinner and Vince's superior at the school—a vile, odious little man named Mr. De Rham—decides to do his Walter Cronkite impressions or, worse, spout off his litany of homophobic jokes.

It's a polite, thin, hollow laugh—perhaps enough to shake the stem of a rhododendron but certainly nothing boisterous enough to rattle the concrete walls of a parking garage. He pulls on his shirt collar as if it were choking him. Overly friendly people have always made Vince retreat no matter the circumstance. Despite his obvious distress, he resumes without the slightest hint of hesitation.

"I'm Vince," he says, "and this is my husband, Terry."

As if commanded by the mere mention of my name, I'm on my feet in a matter of seconds and shaking Lyric's hand. His skin feels rough against mine—coarse and bristly, as if I were shaking hands with a tarantula.

"Nice to meet you," I say, pulling my hand away and disguising my uneasiness by sliding my thumb between my front row of teeth—a loathsome, childish habit I never seemed to break much to my parents' dismay. Lyric's eyebrows furrow at me, as if perplexed by my thumb sucking.

Without hesitation, I yank the thumb from my mouth and scoop Philip from the ground, hoisting him into my arms. "This is our son, Philip."

Lyric releases a deep breath, as if finally comprehending. "Oh, you're a family," he says.

I find myself tensing, waiting for the hammer to finally drop.

"I thought you were brothers," he says.

And there it is.

Vince and I look at one another, passing between us a secret language only we seem to understand. *Not this again*, we silently say to one another, our eyes rolling.

"I'm so sorry," he says. "But you look so alike."

It's a sentiment Vince and I have heard time and time again. If we didn't hold hands or occasionally push our tongues down one another's throats in public, any stranger might assume we were related. I suppose I first fell in love with Vince not only because he adored the parts of me that required more affection and tenderness, but he also mirrored me in so many ways.

Not only was he able to recite Proust down to the punctuation thanks to the finest private school education in Connecticut, but he had the well-practiced forlorn expression of an eighteenth century aristocrat as if pilfered from a portrait by Rembrandt. Of course, it's an expression that has thawed over time as he's entered his forties. However, it's a sadness hidden somewhere deep inside him I cannot help but recognize.

"Honey, come here," Lyric shouts over his shoulder, flagging down a small woman standing on the opposite side of the lawn near the hedges.

She's at his side in a matter of seconds—a petite woman with dark lines creeping at the corners of her eyelids. Her cheeks are caked with rouge as red as clay from desert mountains. Her hair is a mullet of obscene proportions, as if she had lost a bet to her hairdresser.

"This is my wife, Melody," Lyric says, wrapping his arm around her shoulders.

She flashes rows of yellow-stained teeth at us, her lips stretching to form a hideous grin—a smile so exaggerated a clown might be uncomfortable.

"Pleasure to meet you both," she says, offering her left hand.

"Easy name to remember," Lyric says. "A beautiful lyric is nothing without a—"

He leans forward, as if prompting Vince once more.

"Melody," Vince finishes, already clearly exasperated with the phrase as he rests both hands on his hips.

Melody shrieks with excitement, clapping wildly as if she were a mechanical, cymbal-banging monkey. In many ways, she resembles a children's toy—her deadened expressions suddenly springing to life with unmatched verve as if a toddler had pulled a string to animate her. As quickly as vitality comes, it seems to abandon her within a matter of seconds—lips flattening, eyelids shrinking, and eyebrows resting from their otherwise permanent arch.

"Honey," Lyric says, "this is Vince and his husband, Terry."

"How lovely to meet you both," she says, "I thought you were brothers."

Vince and I don't even bother to look at one another once more. We simply fold our arms in unison, as if it were the only guard from their presumptions.

Melody notices Philip dangling from my arms and leans closer. "And who's this little bundle of joy?"

I prop Philip up against my stomach, an arm beneath his bottom and another arm guarding his waist. "This is Philip," I say. "He turned six months yesterday. So, we're celebrating today."

"How exciting," Melody chirps. "May I hold him?"

I stammer at first, eyeing Vince as if hopeful he'll invent some excuse I can't think of right away. He looks at me nonplussed, a soundless question residing in his eyes. "Why are you looking at me like that?" he seems to say without any words. I hope he'll somehow recognize the reluctance pluming all around me, but so far it goes unnoticed. Typical. Vince would allow a pack of mouth-foaming hyenas to have their way with our son if they asked politely enough.

Recognizing I have little to no choice to allow her to hold our child, I merely nod to her. "Of course," I say in the politest tone I can imitate.

I swallow hard, my face souring as if I had just eaten a handful of salt, as I quietly pass Philip from my arms into hers. She receives the precious bundle with wide eyes, careful fingers wrapping around him as his legs dangle from her arms. Philip squirms gently as she pushes him close against her. I can tell he's hating this as much as I am.

I suddenly feel a small pinch on one of my fingers. I look down and I'm greeted by a mosquito perched on my hand, its mouth buried against my skin as it drains me of my blood. I swat at the tiny, winged vampire and it leaps from my hand, circling my head before finally abandoning me.

My attention returns to Melody as she coos at my son, babbling the same baby talk I've read discouraged in the parenting books. Philip seems less than impressed as he rears his head at her as if he were a threatened cottonmouth. Without warning, he spews a generous helping of blended carrots and peas all over Melody's blouse. Then, he starts to cry.

She lurches back, crying out and nearly dropping Philip. I'm quick to intervene, snatching the child from her arms and wiping the amber-colored drool from the corners of his lips.

"I'm so sorry about that," Vince says, guarding Philip and me from her. "We should've warned you. He just ate."

Melody is too distracted with wiping the bits of carrots—as shining as pieces of broken coral—from her flower-printed blouse.

"Oh, that's alright, dear," she says. "These things happen."

She collects the gooey mess in the palm of her hand, suddenly regretting her decision to clean up as she helplessly scans the area for a trash can.

"Do you have a towel she can use?" Lyric asks, spooning the vomit from his wife's hand into his own.

"Yes, of course," Vince says, springing into action and already kneeling down on the blanket to rummage through our picnic basket. Politeness makes a weakling of him yet again. He grabs a handful of napkins and passes them to Lyric and Melody.

They accept the offerings without thanks, Lyric gently patting Melody's neck with the napkin as if he were a painter putting the finishing touches on his masterpiece. When finished, they search us for a response, as if expecting another apology.

"Sorry about that," Vince says. "He usually doesn't get sick. Does he, babe?"

"He's late for his nap," I remind him, propping Philip against my shoulder and resting his bottom in the crutch of my elbow.

"It's OK, dear," Melody says, tucking a used napkin into her pocketbook. "We have a little one, too."

"Do you?" Vince says, the pleasantness of his tone a cheap imitation of something he's probably heard before. "What's his name?"

"Sebastian," Lyric says, pushing his glasses further up his nose. "We named him after the saint. Melody was an admirer of the painting by Il Sodoma. We visited the piece every day at the Palazzo Pitti when we vacationed in Florence."

I know the painting well—the alabaster shimmer of Sebastian's exposed skin, his muscled arms pulled behind his back as if in some form of celestial bondage, the needle-thin arrows skewering his throat and thigh. Although the painting's beauty is unsurpassed, it's not necessarily a piece that might prompt one to consider a child's name. Vince and I had decided to name Philip in honor of Vince's grandfather—a famous Greek pianist.

"Have you been to Florence?" Lyric asks.

Vince's eyes lower for a moment, as if embarrassed and knowing full well a schoolteacher's pittance of a salary will never be enough to take me to Italy one day. "No. We haven't," he says. "But it's on our list."

"Where's your son?" I ask.

Color drains from Lyric and Melody's cheeks, their faces crinkling like drawstring purses, as if bewildered by the question.

Lyric recovers quickly, clearing the catch in his throat. "He's not with us right now."

"Yes. But he will be soon," Melody says, folding her hands as if in prayer. "Very soon, we hope."

"How old is he?" Vince asks, as if oblivious to their obvious discomfort.

I nudge him tenderly. "Here," I say. "Why don't we all sit down and get out of the sun?"

"Very kind of you both," Lyric says, ducking beneath a branch and circling the small, blanketed area we've claimed at the foot of a large Sycamore.

Melody follows her husband, dabbing her shirt with the napkin and cleaning more bits of Philip's lunch from her blouse. I arrange Philip in the pram beside the tree, pulling the sheer canopy over the basket to keep him as cool as possible. He smiles a toothless grin at me, giggling as if he recognizes me. I can only hope he recognizes me.

"He's about—I don't know. What would you say, dear?" Lyric asks, locating a free spot on the blanket and squatting down.

"Who, honey?" she asks.

"Our son."

Melody shakes her head, clearly incensed. "Honestly you don't know how old our boy is?" She coils her arm around mine. Her skin feels damp from a generous helping of sunscreen—it's slippery like the tail of an eel.

"Our son could recite a sonnet by Cavalcanti, and my husband wouldn't say a word," she says to me, dragging me a little closer.

I lead her to a corner of the blanket and sit beside her, my eyes darting between Vince and the pram.

"He's what—?" Lyric says. "Three?"

Melody pulls her pocketbook strap over her shoulder, folding her arms. "He'll be four in two months," she says.

"Four? Already?" Lyric says.

Melody throws him a look that's unmistakable— "You should already know this, asshole," the look seems to say.

"I'm assuming you both adopted," Lyric says, eyeing me and Vince. The word feels weighted— "adopted" —as if it were a concrete brick he had just piled into our arms to carry.

"Terry's best friend from high school actually carried our

child to term," Vince says.

"How wonderful," Melody exclaims, clapping excitedly like a wind-up toy once more. "Isn't it amazing what they can do with modern science?"

"He's our little miracle," I say, reaching out and rubbing Vince's knee with an open palm.

He accepts my tenderness without comment at first. Then, much to my surprise, he pushes my hand away as he swivels toward Lyric.

"So, you were saying I looked like your pen pal?" Vince says.

I feel my cheeks heat with embarrassment. Out of my peripheral vision, I see Melody look at me with concern. I had hoped nobody had played witness to Vince's refusal, but that certainly isn't the case as Lyric quickly scans me for an assessment of the damage as well. However, it's not before long Vince pulls him back into the conversation.

"Yes," Lyric says. "Well, no I mean—not exactly. I've never met him. We've been corresponding since we were in grade school. Started out as an assignment for history class and it's turned into a thirty-year friendship."

"He can't remember his son's birthday, but he can remember to check the mailbox for a new letter every Friday," Melody teases.

They laugh.

I don't.

Instead, my eyes perform a makeshift surgery on my husband—from the broadness of his shoulders to the narrowness of his tapered waist. I split him open in my mind and watch his organs spill out like rotten pieces of fruit. Rummaging through the jewel box of carnage I've arranged in the center of his fileted chest, I search him for the moment it happened—the moment his love for me became an obligation. The horrible moment it no longer was a necessity and instead became a responsibility.

Whether it resides in the marrow of his bones as yellow as amber or whether it's woven into the latticework of his motorway of arteries, the moment exists deep somewhere inside him. Sadly, it's something my hands cannot locate no matter how assiduously my fingers comb through the shining sculpture puzzle of his internal anatomy.

"I thought you might've been him because he says he vacations here from time to time," Lyric says.

"Terry and I moved here after vacationing here for a few years," Vince explains. "Moved out of the city as soon as my job would let me."

"What do you do for work?" Melody asks, her voice thinning.

"I'm a schoolteacher," Vince says. "I teach high school English. Over in New York state."

"Yeah, I saw the out of state plates when you drove in," Lyric says, crossing his legs. Suddenly, realizing what he's said, he pales as if he wishes he could snatch the words hanging from the air. It looks as though his heart has leapt into his throat, his veins bulging as he inhales and exhales.

"You saw us when we drove in?" I ask, my eyes narrowing at him.

Lyric stammers at first, eyes avoiding me at all costs. "I—I noticed the New York plates."

"Lyric loves to play games with the out-of-towners," Melody says, nudging me slightly.

"You're locals though," Lyric says. "So, you don't have to worry."

As he turns his head slightly, I can't help but notice a small earpiece tucked inside his ear. It's the size of a coat button and as glistening black as onyx. On top of the device there's a small red dot flashing a light intermittently as if it were sending out a message in Morse code. I turn my head to face Melody and, secreted beneath her auburn-colored mullet, I notice the same small black earpiece lodged inside her ear as well. The bright red dot flashing a message at me I cannot understand.

"Say, why don't we play a game of Frisbee?" Lyric says, patting my husband on the back. "You play, don't you?"

Vince shrugs, eyeballing me in his peripheral vision. "Well, I haven't in a few—"

"Honey," Lyric says, "Go get the Frisbee out of the picnic basket and bring it over."

Melody is on her feet in a matter of seconds, tugging on my arm. "You'll come play, won't you? You must."

She drags me off the ground, but I'm tethered to the pram. "I have to put the baby down for his afternoon nap," I say. The harder she pulls, the more intensely I hang onto the pram's handle. "I'm sorry."

"Babe, don't worry about him," Vince says, coming to my rescue. "We'll play for a bit and then put him down."

"Wait here. I'll be right back," Melody promises, sprinting out from underneath the tree and across the park's lawn to the small area she and Lyric had claimed near the hedges.

"Come on, guys. Don't leave me hanging," Lyric says, luring us out of the shade.

I check on Philip once more before Vince takes my arm and we inch out from underneath the tree toward Lyric, the afternoon sun swaddling us tightly in a scalding blanket of heat. As we creep across the lawn, I sense Vince's phone vibrate inside his shorts. He digs through his pocket and pulls out his cellphone. The screen lights up with the contact name "Mom" and a picture of Vince and his mother framed in the background. Vince thumbs the "Do not disturb" button, all light vacuumed from the screen.

"You're not going to answer that?" I ask.

"I'll talk to her later," he says, pocketing his phone once more.

Melody arrives with the Frisbee, passing the shining orange disc to her husband.

"Great," Lyric says. "Babe, why don't you go over and stand next to Terry?"

She obliges, galloping over toward me and patting me on the shoulder. "Isn't this fun?" she asks—a question I'm supposed to answer but don't. "Hanging out with you and your husband is no different than hanging out with our other couple friends," she says, smiling from ear to ear. "Especially since Terry's a girl's name."

I feel a slight pinch in the center of my chest and all sound dims around me. Suddenly, I'm returned to the high school locker room—a gang of towel-wrapped adolescents cornering me against my locker and shouting at me, "Terry the fairy." Some of them are larger than me—their generously oiled muscles glinting in the fluorescent lighting as they pummel me with their fists. When they're finished, they grab the nearby laundry cart and dump the soccer team's used uniforms all over me until I'm completely devoured by them.

A voice pulls me out of the giant pile of soiled garments I've arranged in my mind. It's Vince. He calls to me and quite suddenly the locker room is a distant memory, peeling away from me like the skin from a birch tree.

"Babe," he shouts, "stand right where you are. I'll toss it to you. We'll go clockwise."

With the flick of his wrist, he sends the disc sailing into the air toward me. I clutch it between trembling fingers before it smashes into my face. Melody and Lyric applaud wildly, cheering.

"Way to go, Terry," Lyric shouts from across the lawn.

"Pass it to Melody, babe," Vince says.

I pivot slightly, flexing my wrist as I'm about to toss the Frisbee to Melody when Lyric leaps across the lawn, sprinting toward me.

"Wait a minute," he says, circling me until he's behind my back. "Your technique is all wrong."

I deflate, immediately wanting to give up. Sports have never been for me.

"Here. Like this," he says, wrapping his bandaged hand around my waist and cupping my hand with his as we both make contact with the disc.

"Follow my hand," he says, his breath warming the nape of my neck.

I feel him push himself against me as he guides my wrist in one swift motion. He pushes harder against me this time—the roundness of his pectorals, the stiffening of his nipples like metal springs, the firmness of his sculpted abdominals pressing against my spine. My eyes rise to meet Vince's and I notice he's watching us, Lyric pulling me tighter against his body as if he were trying to crawl inside me. He guides my wrist once more, the action ending in a snapping motion. Much to my horror, I sense the front of my pants involuntarily tightening with stiffness as Lyric thrusts against me.

I squirm gently, shrugging out of Lyric's seemingly permanent embrace and swiveling to face him.

"Thanks," I say, my voice a mere whisper. My cheeks redden. "I've never been good at these things."

Lyric flashes me a smile so uncomfortably wide I wonder if his cheeks hurt. Then, he retreats to his side of the lawn and waits.

My eyes return to Vince. He's staring at me, his hands on his hips as if impatient. His eyes narrow to slits, as if signaling a fight to come in the car during the drive home later.

I swallow hard, rotating my hips the way Lyric had taught me as I hurl the Frisbee into the air toward Melody. She leaps from the ground, snatching the disc in mid-air and giggling as she lands on both feet.

"Well done, honey," Lyric shouts, applauding his wife.

Melody leans into the breeze, flinging the Frisbee across the grass toward her husband. He captures it between his fists as if it were a giant winged insect and then hurls it to Vince once more. After several rounds of playing—and one embarrassing trip over a gopher hole—I feel a bead of sweat creep along the shelf of my upper lip. The areas beneath my arms feel wet and sticky, sweat flowering in thick blotches across my shirt. My nostrils flex at the scent of our bodies baking in the afternoon sun—the unpleasant stench of skin roasting in the summer heat.

"I have to check on the baby," I say, reminding Vince.

Vince nods, agreeing. "Yeah. Maybe we should pack it in."

I start making my way back toward the picnic area we had arranged at the base of the Sycamore tree. In the distance, I can see the pram where I had left it, the stuffed animals dangling from the handlebars. Just a few more minutes and this will be over. Vince will think of a way to get rid of them somehow.

"You went to UConn?" Lyric asks my husband as we meander back underneath the shade.

"Yeah. How did you know?"

Lyric points to the short-sleeve T-shirt Vince is wearing, the image of a husky emblazoned in the center of his chest.

"Forgot I was wearing this," Vince says, peeling the shirt from his damp skin.

"I organize a viewing party with a couple of my buddies, usually every Sunday, during the season. You're more than welcome to join," Lyric offers, sliding an arm across Vince's shoulder.

Vince looks to me as if for searching for approval, but I look away.

"Sure. I'd love to," he says.

"Great." Lyric whips out his cellphone, slides a finger across his screen and passes the device to Vince. "Put in your number."

Vince's fingers flick across the screen, typing. When finished, he hands the phone back to Lyric.

"I'll text you," Lyric says.

We reach the small blanket arranged beneath the tree and I'm quick to trot over to the pram, lifting the sheer canopy arranged over the mouth of the basket. It's then that my vision becomes blurry, my heart hammering against the plate of my chest.

I recognize the awful truth—Philip is gone.

His stuffed owl named Boris remains tossed in the corner of the basket. The blankets are draped in a large pile as if hastily discarded during the raid.

I clutch my throat, trying to speak but it feels as though my throat were tinged with salt and ash.

"Babe?" Vince says, drawing closer and reaching out to grab me.

I stagger away from the empty pram, my knees buckling as I make the slightest movement. The world around me seems to quiver as if everything were constructed of gelatin, all sounds blurring together until it's a deafening drone that only a hive of bees could compare. I'm yanked to the ground, mouth open as if a fishing hook were caught in my jaw.

Vince skirts across the blanket and comes upon the empty basket, his eyes widening with horror at the sight.

"Oh my God," he says, covering his mouth. "We have to call the police."

"What's happened?" Lyric asks, his face hardening with seriousness.

Vince merely points to the empty pram.

"Yes. We know," Lyric says with the same matter-of-fact ease of when he had first greeted us.

Vince turns mechanically, eyebrows furrowing at him. "You know—?"

I sense the words crawling up my throat as if they were armored beetles, creeping out from between my lips. "Where is he?"

"I suggest you don't call the police," Lyric says. "Especially if you want to see your boy again."

Vince looks around like an animal with a limb caught in a steel-trap—frightened, helpless. "What the fuck did you do to him?"

"We didn't do anything to him," Melody says. "But they'll hurt him if you don't do what we say."

My stomach curls at the mere thought of Philip drowsing in

unfamiliar, uncaring arms. I scan the area—from the young couples milling about the towering hedges on the opposite side of the lawn to the children playing near the fountain arranged on a small terrace made from marble near the park's main entrance.

Philip is nowhere in sight.

The surrounding noises of summertime merriment—the sounds of children shouting as they play, young lovers laughing as they stroll with bodies pressed lovingly against one another—all seem like insults to my agony: my bright, enchanted suffering.

"Where the fuck is he?" Vince's fists tighten, as if he's planning to make good use of them.

"Maybe we should sit down?" Lyric suggests, crumpling to both knees.

"Calm down first," Melody adds, joining her husband on the ground and folding her legs the same way a child does.

I watch Vince as he pulls out his cellphone, his trembling fingers sliding across the screen.

"I'm calling the police," he says.

"They'll kill him," Lyric says, his voice firming with urgency. He looks at Vince, his quarter-sized pupils seeming to beg him to put the phone away. His voice softens slightly—another father's reassurance. "Please. I'm on your side."

Vince's fingers pause from dialing the three numbers. His eyes scour Lyric, as if poking through the brawn of his anatomy for the truth. "Who are they?"

"Sit. Please," Lyric begs, motioning. He's no longer smiling but rather executing every movement with rehearsed formality as if his every action were being studied and graded by some distant observer.

I look at Vince for encouragement, as if a mere look from him will protect me from the torment sweltering inside me. However, I go wanting for any semblance of safety as Vince's eyes remain trained on Lyric the same way a predator stalks their prey.

Vince pockets his phone, kneeling to meet Lyric at eye level. I sense my knees quivering as I bend down alongside him, slight pressure tightening inside my pelvis as if I have to pee. I cross my legs as if I were tying a knot in a garden hose, the pressure slowly subsiding.

"Where is he?" Vince demands, his lips crimping like the edges of an untreated wound.

"We're going to play a game," Lyric says, his voice stilted, wooden as if he were reciting the words from memory. "If you follow our directions, you'll be reunited with your son."

Vince leaps up from kneeling, his fingers already back on his phone screen to dial. "I'm not playing this fucking game."

Melody swats at him, pleading. "Please. They'll kill him if you don't do what we say."

Her eyes are wet and shining. I recognize the shrill sound of fear clogging in her throat as if an invisible hand were squeezing her neck with the intent to kill. She smears the snot dripping from her nose, the pitiful expression of a penniless market beggar making its home across her face—the drooping eyelids, the trembling lips crinkling downward. For the first time since we've met them, I believe what she says—they will kill our child if we don't listen to them.

I tug on Vince's hand. He flinches at my touch. "Please. Listen to them."

Vince seems to slacken, his shoulders dropping and his arms falling at his side—whether his weakening is from momentary relief or hopelessness, I'm uncertain. Regardless, he kneels once more and trains his eyes on Lyric.

"Now, the rules are simple," Lyric says, the preciseness of his every word flinging tiny daggers at me with the prowess of a skilled marksman until I'm an impaled effigy of my former self—a grotesque tribute to a fresco depicting the glorious destruction of a virgin martyr. "I ask you both to tell me five of the most horrible, most shameful things you've done in your life—your worst secrets for the Party Guest."

"Who?" Vince asks.

"Someone watching us right now," Lyric says.

My head immediately swivels as if my neck were built upon an elastic coil, scanning the lawn for a person, a sign—anything. My eyes dart between parents toting their children as they meander through the gardens and bicyclists shooting down the nearby trail—their garishly colored outfits flickering behind a curtain of small trees.

"If the Party Guest decides you're lying, or cheating in any way, we'll have to take our necessary penance."

Vince seems fearful to ask. "What kind of penance?"

"A finger," Lyric says. "A finger for every secret."

"Whoever has the most fingers remaining wins," Melody adds, as if it were any consolation.

"Wins what?" Vince asks.

"Afraid we can't say," Lyric says. "But since you asked you can go first."

Lyric straightens, rising from his seat and circling Vince the way a carnivore might stalk a smaller animal. "Now, tell me one of your most shameful memories from childhood," he says. "Speak loudly so the Party Guest can hear."

I search the nearby area for a sign once more—perhaps a park visitor with a cellphone glued to their ear, listening to us. I see an elderly man—thick briars of ashen grey hair bulging from beneath a fedora—sitting on a nearby bench with a cellphone pinned against his ear. I watch him for a moment, my eyes narrowing at him, until I see him hang up and slowly rise to greet his wife with an embrace.

I comb the area again for another hint, another clue—anything to reveal the puppet master of this exercise in torture. In the distance, I see a middle-aged man, his gut drooping over the belted waistband of his khaki shorts, aiming a pair of binoculars at us.

Finally.

I've caught him.

I'm about to grab Vince and point when I realize the man is merely focusing his set of binoculars on a small family of sparrows gathered in the nearby grass to feed.

Vince looks at me with hesitation, almost as if he's preparing me for an answer I don't want to hear.

"Well?" Lyric prompts.

Vince swallows hard. "When I was little, I cheated on an assignment. I leaned over my desk and copied the answers from the boy sitting next to me. Got an A on the test."

Lyric pushes the earpiece further inside his ear, as if he's listening to someone speak. He waits for a moment, the faint hiss of a voice speaking to him. Removing his finger from the earpiece, he approaches Vince with distinct somberness as if he were addressing an inmate on the night of their execution.

"I'm sorry," he says, "But, the Party Guest isn't buying your story."

Vince's mouth hangs open, as if desperately trying to

comprehend.

"I—I don't—"

For the first time in my life, Vince appears smaller than he actually is,—as though all the air had been sucked out of him through a valve as tiny as a pinhole on the top of his head.

Out of the corner of my eye, I watch as Melody searches in between the giant roots of the overhanging Sycamore, her hands going in between the wooden veins spiderwebbing across the earth's floor. Finally, she locates what she's looking for—a large rock with jagged edges. She brandishes it as though it were a holy relic to be worshipped.

"He's asked me to make it right," Lyric explains.

Without warning, Lyric leaps on top of Vince like a livid primate and holds his shoulders down. Vince resists, struggling against the bulk of Lyric's weight, but he's too heavy. Melody grabs my husband's hand, pressing his open palm against the ground and spreading his fingers apart.

"Wait—" I say. The word is a poor excuse for any semblance of a defense, but it's the only one I have.

"I'm so sorry," she says, her eyes plotting the labor at hand.

She raises the rock high above her head. But, before she brings it down, her eyes meet mine and everything around us seems to slow to a halt. She looks as if she's rethinking everything, her grip visibly weakening. I silently beg her to put the rock down—a fellow parent's plea to reconsider and make this all go away.

But, before another moment of hesitation, her hand makes the decision for her. She drives the rock down and smashes the jagged edge against Vince's index finger. A wet, crunching sound as his bone snaps apart as if it were a mere pencil. He cries out like a wounded animal, jaw hanging open in disbelief.

I cover my mouth at the sight, my scream muted.

Lyric adds more pressure on my husband, straining against him as Melody removes the rock and reveals Vince's broken finger—the knuckle bruised purple and already beginning to swell. In a final stroke to decide the matter, Melody raises the rock and hammers it down once more against Vince's finger. He howls in agony, and Lyric tightens his arm around his throat and covers his mouth to stifle him.

I watch as the finger finally separates as though it were made of damp cotton, an exquisite scarlet plant blooming from the exposed tissue when Melody slides the severed digit away from Vince's hand and wraps it in a cloth.

Lyric fishes inside his pocket and reveals a wad of bandages. He starts wrapping Vince's hand with them, pressing hard against the wound and causing Vince to jerk in agony as if he were a puppet. Melody grabs some of the dressings from her husband and passes a handful to me.

"Here," she says. "You'll need these later."

Just as I'm about to take the bandages from her, I notice a man in brightly colored running gear sprinting toward us. Lyric and Melody stiffen, turning their backs to him as if they were reprimanded school children.

"If you say one word, they'll kill him," Lyric promises, pressing his lips against my husband's ear.

The man slows as he approaches us, lifting his glasses and wiping the sweat smeared across his forehead. He hides a look of concern beneath a polite smile as he comes upon our little group.

"Is everything OK over here?" he asks, his eyes meeting my gaze.

This is my moment, I think to myself. *My chance to get help.*

Right when I'm about to open my mouth, Melody presses a cellphone against my ear and shouts, "Dear, it's Philip. Listen."

I pull the phone closer, hearing a child screech through a garbled hiss of static. "Philip? Baby?"

Out of my peripheral hearing, I listen to Lyric engage with the man as he coddles my husband as if he were a wounded child.

"Just a little accident," Lyric explains. "Cut his finger slicing apples."

The man's face sours when he notices the blood pooling beneath my husband's hastily wrapped bandage. "Do you need me to get some help? That looks pretty bad."

Lyric adds pressure to Vince's hand, more blood leaking out and Vince shriveling in pain at his touch. "We're going to take him to the hospital right now."

"Want me to call an ambulance?" the man asks, brandishing his cellphone.

"It's alright, buddy," Lyric assures him. "We'll make sure he's OK. Thanks."

The man looks at me as if for reassurance, but I'm far too

distracted listening to the sounds of Philip chirping excitedly on the other end of the line.

"Philip?" I say, as if somehow hoping he'll respond. "It's Daddy."

But, suddenly, there's no response. The connection has been severed.

I watch as the man slides his eyeglasses up his nose, pocketing his cellphone. "You folks have a nice afternoon," he says, adjusting his wristwatch before sprinting off down the nearby path.

"You too," Lyric calls out to him as the man disappears. "Enjoy this beautiful weather."

Without warning, Melody snatches the phone from my ear and slips it back inside her pocketbook, casketing the remainder of my hope. I watch as Lyric leans over my husband, pushing the earpiece further inside his ear once more as if intently listening.

"The Party Guest sends his compliments," he says. "Well done."

Melody lifts the lid to the portable ice box and tosses Vince's severed finger wrapped in cloth inside, a blast of icy air cooling us for a moment.

"Shall we continue?" she says, eyeing her husband as if hopeful.

Lyric regards me like an auctioneer who's just made a sale. "It's your turn," he says to me.

Melody grips the blood-soaked rock, eyeing my hand as if preparing for her next labor. I sense my fingers curling into a fist as I watch Lyric sprawl himself out on the blanket in front of me. A quick punch to the jaw and he'd be flat on his back like an expired cockroach. But then what would I do? I don't know where they've taken Philip. Besides, they've promised time and time again he'll be hurt if we don't follow their game accordingly.

I curse myself for being so distracted by Melody's phone call when the runner had checked on us—an opportunity to save my family and I let it slip away. I wonder to myself if that was even Philip who I had heard on the other end of the line. Perhaps it was his kidnapper crudely imitating a child's laugh. Perhaps Philip has already been killed—the very last breath of life squeezed from between his crimpled lips, his overalls torn and tattered as he lies face down on a cushion of shining black trash bags.

There must be someone else around who can help, I think to myself.

I scan the nearby park visitors once more, searching for anyone who appears as if they can sense my distress. Surrounded by others and yet I've never felt so alone.

Lyric wrenches my attention back to him with the sound of his voice. "The Party Guest is waiting," he says.

I stiffen, my heart leaping into my throat. "Yes."

Biding my time, I search my mind for a recollection—something revealing enough to satisfy him, but not so exposing that I'm humiliated once more. Finally, it comes to me.

"I have one," I say.

"We're listening," Lyric says, folding his arms as if preparing to be disappointed.

"I was climbing a tree with one of my classmates one day," I say. "I was the better climber. So, I had the lead. I remember scampering up the tree and looking back down at my friend as he continued to crawl up, struggling. I remember wanting to see him fall. So, I leaned against a branch, pulled my dick through my zipper, and started peeing on him. He laughed nervously. But I never told him that I wanted to humiliate him—that I wanted to see him suffer."

My words hang in the air like broken dreamcatchers—their webbing ripped apart and their beads smashed like bits of hard candy. I find myself avoiding eye contact with my husband, but I can feel his eyes boring holes in me the size of duck eggs, as if begging me to look at him.

I don't.

Instead, my eyes are fixed on Lyric as he presses against the earpiece, listening intently for a moment.

"Well done," he finally says to me.

Melody exhales in relief, her grip loosening on the rock already greased with Vince's blood. There's clearly a part of her—hidden, camouflaged behind the rhapsodic smiles and the vigorous applause—that questions her brutality. If only I could find it, drag it screaming out of her and hold it by its very root as if it were some monstrous plant nestled deep inside her.

"Your turn again," Lyric says to Vince, pouring himself a glass of lemonade from the pitcher.

I watch as Vince seems to retreat deep inside himself, his arms and legs shortening as if he were trying to pull himself out of his skin like coat sleeves. His eyes wander to his bandaged hand, an empty space where his index finger should be. He looks as though he's rehearsing the words in his head at first, his lips moving with muted sounds.

Lyric downs the glass of lemonade. He pours another one, signaling to his wife if she wants a glass. She shakes her head.

"When I was little, I went on vacation with my parents," Vince says, carefully going over each word. "And when we were driving in the taxi from the airport, I found a grasshopper beneath the seat. So, I decided to tuck the little insect inside my mother's hair as she sat in front of me. A day went by and one night I woke up to my mother screaming, my dad rooting through her hair. I guess the grasshopper I had found was pregnant and had delivered her babies on top of my mother's head."

I shiver slightly, my head itching as though I can sense miniature limbs crawling through my hair. Out of the corner of my eye, I see Melody scratch her head as if she, too, feels the tingle of tiny legs working their way across her skull—little emerald bodies burrowing through thick brambles of hair, feeding and nesting.

Once more, the unseen Party Guest is satisfied according to Lyric and it's my turn again.

"Something a bit more daring perhaps," Lyric says, his tongue flicking out and slicing me as if there were a knife buried beneath it.

"Like what?" I say.

"Something you've never told your husband," he says.

I think for a moment, mind racing. Finally. Another one comes to me.

"When I was five or six, I was cutting out construction paper with my little brother," I say. "I remember looking at his fingers and wondering what would happen if I cut the tip of his finger. So, I slid his finger between the blade and clamped down. I remember my mother screaming, holding my little brother's hand beneath the kitchen sink faucet."

I cup my hands, wringing my fingers as if I could somehow undo their damage. I feel as though I'm on the verge of breaking apart—an already cracked windshield slammed by a sudden gust of wind. I can scarcely control myself, shoving my finger between my lips and sucking with force, as if to remind myself I'm still fully intact.

My eyes meet Vince's. He doesn't seem to regard me with disdain but rather indifference at the sight of my teeth clenching down and my cheeks sucking in as I nurse on my thumb. I feel a tremor of disgrace settle deep inside me the same way a frog buries itself in the mud during the winter months.

Lyric listens to his earpiece, a voice stretching its fingers through his head and snaking its way through his eardrum like the body of a centipede. Then, he nods at Melody. The fist she's made around the rock loosens for the time being.

"Why are you doing this?" Vince asks, glistening beads of sweat collecting at his hairline.

Lyric and Melody do not answer. They merely glare at him like siblings of the same inevitable sorrow; a sorrow we, too, will soon presumably understand.

"How long are we going to keep doing this?" Vince asks, his voice thinning to a whisper.

Lyric drums his fingers against the lid of the picnic basket. "It's your turn."

Vince draws in a labored breath, thinking.

"When I was six years old, I was playing a game with my older brother," he says. "He scared me, and I shit myself by accident. So, I took my soiled underwear and I stuffed it inside a crack in the attic wall. But it started to smell and eventually the entire house smelled like shit."

Vince looks at me for a moment before hanging his head, his eyes lowering in humiliation.

"It got so bad that my parents tried selling the house, but nobody would buy it," he says, eyes avoiding all of us at every cost. "It was my fault. I never told them."

Lyric listens to his earpiece. Then, a thumbs up.

"Terry," he says, prompting me. "Your turn."

But I'm too indignant to be complicit any longer. I vault from my seat and I'm at Lyric's face in seconds. "I need to see my son."

Lyric preserves his composure, gently wetting his lips. "I told you. If you do what we say, you'll see him again. Sooner rather than later."

"No. That's not good enough," I say. "I want him now."

"You'll leave us alone if we finish the game?" Vince asks.

"Of course," Vince says.

"Like we told you," Melody adds.

Vince's eyes pull me to meet his. He wrenches my attention to his wounded hand—the blood still leaking from his severed finger. "Just finish the game, Terry," he says. "They'll leave us alone."

I want to believe him. But I feel so lost, as if I were a small woodland creature displaced to the rolling dunes of a distant desert. Quieting my verve, I resume my seat beside Melody. Everyone looks at me, expectant.

"When I was little, I was bullied every day at school," I say. "One day, a girl called me a 'faggot' and ran off with her friends, laughing. So, I grabbed a pinecone from the ground and threw it at her. But she turned around when I threw it and it hit her in the eye. The parents didn't press charges, thankfully. But that was the day my parents first called me a 'monster.'"

I wait for a sign from Lyric as he pushes the earpiece inside his ear, listening to the Party Guest. He flashes a smile at me, nodding.

"Well done," he says to me, adjusting his glasses. "Now, the Party Guest wants something more recent. Something you haven't shared with one another." His eyes narrow at me. "You start, Terry," he says.

I scarcely know where to begin. Of course, I know what to say; however, I hardly expected to ever share this with Vince, least of all perfect strangers. I regard Lyric and Melody with caution, as if brutality is not their only talent, and that they've somehow been endowed with the gift of telepathy as well.

"I was in high school and I was dating a girl named Clara," I say. "Everybody in school kept telling her I was gay, and she started to believe them. So, to prove it to myself and to her that I wasn't, we made love on prom night."

I shudder at the recollection of our sweating bodies pressed together, unsure hands groping for the sake of pleasure and curiosity.

"But, a few weeks later, she came to me and told me she was pregnant," I say. "I begged her to get rid of it." I wipe the dampness from my eyes as I choke on quiet sobs. "And she did. She got rid of it because I asked her to."

My eyes flicker to Vince, hopeful for a semblance of

reassurance. But he won't look at me, his eyes instead trained on the ground in front of him.

Lyric nods, visibly content with my agony. "Well done," he says to me. Then, he motions to Vince. "Your turn."

Vince lowers his head for a moment, his shoulders drooping as if preparing for something. He resembles the tattered remains of a scarecrow after a windstorm—straw pulled out from broken limbs like intestines made of confetti.

"When I was in college, I got a perfect score on an essay about the subject of racism in Shakespeare's plays," Vince says. "But I didn't deserve the grade. Because I had plagiarized the entire essay." His eyes search me, as if for an explanation. "How can I be a role model for my students if I did the very thing I tell them not to do?"

Lyric brings his hand to his ear once more, listening to the voice whispering inside the earpiece. He smiles, flashing Vince a thumbs up.

"Now, it's our last party trick," he says. "Our host is convinced you both have saved the best for last." His eyes immediately snap to me. "Terry—?"

I tighten as if he's just lassoed me with a rope until I'm nothing more than bound cattle. I retreat deep inside myself, searching for a confession. Nothing comes to me. Lyric and Melody eye me with their scrupulous gaze, pulling me back to the blood-soaked picnic blanket in the shade.

"I . . . don't have one," I murmur, my voice delicate.

"You're certain?" Lyric asks. "You know the penance for lying."

"I'm not lying," I say. "I have nothing left to give."

Lyric's eyes lower, confessing a genuine disappointment at the inevitable task at hand as he motions to Melody to retrieve the rock once more. She does, taking my hand and splaying my fingers across the ground in preparation. I sense my heart flutter slightly, marveling at the rock as she holds it—the jagged edges, the tapered point to effortlessly hack through bone.

I don't resist the way I thought I might. Instead, I merely surrender, my every extremity deadening with numbness. The world around us seems to slow, a blast of heat washing over me as if it were a tidal wave.

I see Vince watching me as Melody raises the rock above her

shoulders, about to bring it down.

He leaps up from his seat, shouting, "Wait."

Melody freezes, the rock held high above her head as if she were a bronzed replica of a star athlete mid-play.

"I have something that will make up for both of us," Vince says, his head falling in obvious shame. "Something . . . I've never told my husband. Something that would ruin me if anyone ever found out."

Melody looks to her husband for approval. Once he nods to her, agreeing, she loosens her grip about the rock and sets it down beside her.

Vince stands motionless for a moment, as if he were deciding where to begin. I wonder if he'll bolt, leave me with Lyric and Melody, and run somewhere to get help. It would be over, then. But who knows if we'd ever see Philip again?

He inhales deeply, the sound of his breath whistling.

"For the past four months, I've been telling Terry I've been staying after school to help tutor kids in my AP English class," he says. "But instead, I've been meeting with just one student named Derek. He and I . . . have been meeting at the motor lodge on Route 7 in Cornwall."

I cover my mouth, involuntarily releasing a sound like a dying animal—a pathetic creature on the verge of death as their continence abandons them.

"It was never supposed to go on for this long," he explains, his eyes begging me for an absolution I'll never dispense. "I meant to cut it off so many times."

"How old is he?" Lyric asks—a question I wish he hadn't.

Vince looks at me, his face flushed with embarrassment. "Seventeen."

I double over as if I'm about to vomit, a pain working its way through my viscera—the giant hand of a deity pushing through my innards and squeezing out the last breath from my lungs.

"What else?" Lyric asks, as if knowing full well there's more.

"I . . . disguised his phone number as my mom's number so Terry wouldn't find out," Vince says.

I muffle a soft cry into a fist as I cover my mouth again.

Lyric leans back, pressing his finger against the earpiece as he listens. His eyes flick to his wife, a smile creeping across his face.

"It's over, baby," he says.

Melody slackens, releasing a breath. Words she's obviously been waiting for.

"Where is he?" she asks, frantically scanning the area for something—someone.

Lyric's cellphone chirps. He slides his fingers across the screen, then presses it against his ear, listening. A few moments later and he hangs up, pointing across the way to the fountain arranged near the park's entrance.

"He's by the fountain," he says, leaping off the ground.

Melody follows, tossing the rock aside.

"Wait," Vince says. "What about our son? You promised."

As if suddenly remembering, Lyric passes Vince a wad of extra bandage. Then, he removes his earpiece and tosses it to Vince.

"You'll need these," he says.

Melody does the same, removing her earpiece and pressing the small device into my open palm.

Once they're finished bestowing their gifts, they abandon us as quickly as they arrived, sprinting across the lawn toward the large fountain near the park's entrance. My eyes follow them and it's then I notice a small boy—no older than three or four—dressed in a plaid shirt and wearing a propeller hat waving to them as he stands beside the fountain. Lyric and Melody are on him in a matter of seconds, swallowing him in an embrace and pecking him with kisses.

My mouth hangs open, desperately trying to comprehend.

Then, as if on cue, Vince's cellphone rings. He stares at the screen, unblinking—an anonymous number. He looks at me, hopeful I'll answer it. When I'm not as compliant as he hopes, he swipes one of his remaining fingers across the screen and holds the phone to his ear.

"Hello?" His breath shakes.

A peculiar voice greets him on the other end of the line—brittle, thin as if it were the sound of a dying insect.

"You played an excellent game," the voice tells him. "I have a notion you'll be exceptional in the Captain's chair."

"Where is he?" Vince asks, the veins in his neck bulging.

"You'll see him again," the voice says. "He's safe only if you follow our rules."

Vince crumples to his knees as if the wind had been sucked

out of him. "Why are you doing this?"

"Do you see those earpieces?" the voice asks. "Put them on. Both of you."

Vince slides the earpiece into his ear and motions to me to do the same. As soon as I do, the strange voice fills my eardrum.

"Can you hear me?" it asks.

We nod in unison.

"Good."

Vince's head swivels around, his face flushing as if he were about to burst into flames. "Where the fuck are you?"

"Now, your name is Lyric," the voice says to Vince. "Your husband's name is Melody. A beautiful lyric is nothing without a melody, after all. And vice versa. Do you understand?"

"Please," Vince begs. "We just want our son back."

"And you'll get him back," the voice promises. "As long as you follow my directions. I'll wager you wouldn't want your confession to be sent to the authorities."

Vince falls silent, as if the stranger's voice had snatched the very root of his tongue from his mouth.

"Very good," the voice says.

"What do you want?" Vince asks.

"You're to find another young couple with a child," the voice says. "Approach them and merely say, 'You're not supposed to be here.' I'll instruct you to do the rest when the time comes."

The line suddenly disconnects.

Vince regards me with a look of bewilderment—the same way a masked surgeon might address the loved ones of a patient who had died on the operating table.

Vince might as well be a complete stranger now—his every molecule a secret to me.

I rise from my seat, anticipating the inevitable—our game far from finished.

I scan the nearby area, this time not for help, but rather for a victim. I'm a cottonmouth in hiding—a cobra threatening to strike. My eyes are immediately pulled to a young couple spread out on a checkered blanket arranged near a row of rose bushes. The young man—perhaps carrying a few more extra pounds than he should, the silhouette of a star high school athlete buried somewhere beneath his flab—stretches himself in the sun. His wife—her petite frame outfitted in a paisley summer dress—lies on her back with their child straddling her stomach and laughing.

I point them out to Vince. He seems to nod in agreement.

We begin to make our way over to them, ducking out of the shade and into the heat of the summer sun once more.

He goes to touch my hand as we walk, but I pull away.

Vince doesn't matter right now.

Only Philip does—finding him, bringing him home.

In a matter of seconds, we're at the edge of the young couple's picnic blanket, staring down at them—unannounced visitors, omens of destruction.

They regard us with friendly smiles. For once, I envy the cheeriness of the ignorant—smiles so broad and revealing it looks as though their faces might split in half. Very soon they won't be smiling. Very soon their child will be missing—screams at the realization of his absence, sobbing, pleading—and then we'll be their captors, announcers of their humiliation.

I suddenly regard them, not if they were human beings, but rather as if their bodies were the undisturbed archaeological sites of ancient tombs—the secrets they must protect in their darkest recesses, the unrevealed confessions lying dormant inside them like the jeweled remains of long-since deceased Pharaohs.

I wonder what they are, what they could possibly be.

Part of me is eager to find out.

"You're not supposed to be here," Vince quietly says to them as if it were a warning, a final admonition, like the sky turning as green as seawater before a summer storm.

WHERE FLAMES
BURNED EMERALD AS
GRASS

"PERDÓN SEÑOR?" HE CALLED, FLAGGING down
one of the hotel's immaculately groomed waitstaff from across
the pool with an embroidered white handkerchief.

Nearly three weeks in the heart of the Costa Rican rainforest
and the integrity of Norval Dowling's Spanish accent remained
as unrefined as bulldozed bedrock. Certainly, much could be said
of his methodically calculated attempts to resemble a formal
tourist in such a laid-back climate—his high-waisted khaki shorts
with breathable mesh lining to keep him cool during the
afternoon's usual mugginess, his anti-theft waist band secured
around his hips where he stored his credit cards and passport,
and his handmade puttees wrapped around his ankles to prevent
venomous insects from crawling inside his footwear.

Although he had made every effort to indoctrinate his nine-
year-old daughter Cassie into his expertly designed regimen, she
remained less than willing to comply. To him she was merely a
loathsome free spirit as he exasperatedly watched her circle laps
in the pool without the proper eyewear.

"I told her to wear her goggles," he said as soon as the

bemused server arrived at his table.

The server recoiled almost instantly, guarding himself with the empty silver platter, as if he were intruding upon a private moment between father and daughter.

"Cass," Norval shouted at his daughter as he leaned forward in his cushioned seat, brandishing a pair of purple goggles she had abandoned beside his plate. "Your eyewear. For protection. You don't know what's been in that water."

But, as was her custom, she pretended not to hear him, floating further away from the pool's shallow end and toward the Pruitt children treading in the deeper water. Of course, Norval had no objection to his daughter fraternizing with the Pruitt twins—a pair of young ladies no older than twelve and dressed in identical yellow bathing suits. After all, they came from a fine pedigree as one of the oldest lineages still maintaining residence in Newtown, Connecticut, and over the course of their stay at The Flornegra Resort & Spa, Norval had become friendly with their parents, Eva and Richard. Regardless, it was an embarrassment to be ignored by his child even in front of a perfect stranger.

"She probably didn't hear me," he muttered to the waiter, eyes lowering to the papers scattered across the table in front of him as color filled his cheeks.

"Something to drink, señor? Un refresco?"

"Si," Norval said, straightening himself, as if he were priming the invisible and dangerously shallow fountain of Spanish words at his mind's disposal.

Eyes squinting, he immediately referred to his small travel book where he had scrawled Spanish words and phrases to use when ordering. "Me gustaría un café con hielo."

The waiter simpered, amused by the atrociousness of Norval's Spanish accent. Recovering quickly, the waiter bowed.

"Si, señor," he said, clearing the small plates of half-eaten fruit empanadas from in front of Norval before whisking them away to the kitchenette adjoining the cabana on the opposite side of the pool.

Norval's ears perked at the sounds of something scurrying above him, the gentle pitter-patter of feet dashing to and from both sides of the vine-draped trellis canopying him from the afternoon sun.

He raised his head, squinting as sunlight flickered through the robes of greenery hanging above him, and he saw a small primate—a Capuchin monkey with a sorrowful childlike face framed inside a bonnet of white fur—leaping from handle to handle of the poolside grotto's wooden latticework.

Norval watched in amusement as the small monkey scampered down the rope of vines, tail curling as it screeched excitedly to its brethren tucked away in the surrounding dangling greenery. Norval's amusement, however, ended soon after the primate rocketed onto his table and began to make itself more comfortable among Norval's possessions. Norval swiped the papers he had scattered about the table as the monkey pecked at the empanada crumbs discarded on the tablecloth. He snatched the napkin folded across his lap and waved it at the primate, as if a feeble attempt to shoo it away. The monkey remained unaffected, its tiny fingers searching the table for unwanted food remnants.

It wasn't long before the small primate eyed the papers clutched in Norval's fist, swiping at them with its paws and cooing. Norval retreated slightly, leaning back in his seat as the tiny aggressor clawed at him and cried for backup from perhaps more virile family members watching the scene play out from the vine-draped awning above. Without warning, the monkey seized one of the papers from Norval's fist and launched from the table onto one of the vines swaying beside him. Norval leapt out of his seat, lunging after the miniature trespasser. But he wasn't quick enough as the monkey vaulted up the rope and finally came to a halt when it reached the handlebar at the summit of the trelliswork.

Norval jumped, arms flailing to swipe the paper from the monkey's paws, but it was no use. The monkey, grinning sheepishly, began to rip apart the paper and toss the tattered pieces down to the ground from the comfort of his perch. Norval raced to collect the torn pieces of paper as they were sent floating down to him—some of the pieces were bitten apart or chewed on. He figured fitting the scraps back together was no use. When the monkey had finally deserted the final shred of paper, angrily tossing it down to Norval like a toddler abandoning a toy that wouldn't properly work, it scampered off and vanished into the surrounding greenery.

Norval stooped to one knee, collecting the tattered bits in his hands and going over each piece as he struggled to decipher what he had written. It might not have been such a tragedy if the damned thing had snatched the most recent page he was working on, but the monkey had ravaged the very first page of Norval's eleven-page (and counting) letter. Damned if he could remember what he had written on the first page since he first began writing the letter last night at eleven. His shoulders drooped, knowing for certain he'd have to start all over again.

Of course, he could have used the hotel lobby's computer for the sake of easier file recovery. Then again, he hardly expected his writing to be ripped apart quite literally by a territorial primate. Besides, there was something so incredibly romantic about the art of handwriting a letter—especially when it was intended to be sent to his lover. There was something so exhilarating in the act of surreptitiously writing a letter longhand—a letter to someone his daughter didn't even know about.

As Norval returned to his chair and brandished his fountain pen, he wondered if she ever would. Of course, he reasoned she must have expected he would eventually move on after the death of her mother nearly three years ago; however, he figured his daughter hardly ever anticipated his father would stray from the fairer sex and instead find comfort in the arms of a gentleman.

He had already wasted so many sleepless nights envisioning how he might tell her, how he might broach the subject. It was one thing to move on and find companionship in another partner; however, it was an entirely different matter to subject his innocent daughter to his identity crisis. Revealing the truth behind his relationship felt like a monstrous confession—a ghastly betrayal—more than anything else.

Moreover, he wondered if it might be an insult to the memory of his deceased wife. He lovingly gazed at the tattoo just visible beneath the hem of his sleeve on his right bicep—an intricately drawn black-and-white portrait of his wife with the date of her death, "December 12th," inscribed below her image. Although he reasoned that three years was a longer amount of time than the lifespan of some pet mice, he certainly couldn't reconcile with the fact that it wasn't a long enough amount of time to dishonor twelve years of marriage.

Then again, his lover Ali had been more than patient with him as he struggled to navigate the situation. He wondered if that's what he had written on the first page of the letter—perhaps a litany of gratitude to Ali for his unwavering patience. Norval wondered if perhaps he had spent the first page of the letter confessing to frivolous peccadillos, like the fact that he often avoids sleeping on his left side because it wears the heart out quicker according to a black-and-white film he had once seen. Or perhaps he had simply written of missing Ali, especially the birthmark on his inner left thigh.

Whatever the contents of the tattered page contained, Norval reasoned it was for the best the letter was destroyed. After all, he and his daughter had been in Costa Rica for several weeks now, and he conceded he had spent much more time devoted to secretly penning letters to his loved one than interacting with Cassie. Moreover, the letters being written in return by Ali were becoming few and far between. Norval wondered if perhaps Ali was losing interest or becoming exasperated with the waiting game.

Even then, the thought of losing Ali didn't necessarily prompt Norval to reconsider telling Cassie of their affair. As he stirred in his seat, tapping the tip of the fountain pen on his pad of paper, he watched his daughter in the pool from a distance. She leapt out of the water, splashing one of the Pruitt twins and clearly annoying them. As he watched her, he couldn't help but feel saddened at the prospect of the many rites of womanhood she'll have to endure without a mother. He knew for certain he wouldn't be able to guide her the way her mother could have.

Recalling the moment when he uncovered bloodstained tissues and underwear in the laundry, Norval's heart nearly leapt out of his chest at the memory. Once again unsure how to even present the subject without the added uncomfortableness, he recalled how he had purchased a box of tampons and left them out on the bathroom counter and hoped she knew how to use them. Of course, they hadn't discussed the awkward moment nor the bloodstained indiscretions since they first occurred. Regardless, Norval wished he were able to provide everything for Cassie her mother could not.

Watching as she scaled the small ladder in the deeper end of the pool, Norval saw his daughter hurl herself onto the deck and squeezed her hair out to dry. She waved at the Pruitt twins who remained treading in the water, as if motioning to them that she would be right back. On the peripheral of his vision, Norval caught sight of another Capuchin monkey scampering across the vined canopy hanging over the pool. This one, larger than the other and seemingly even more dominant, leapt from vine to vine and eventually began to climb down one of the ropes dangling beside Cassie.

Norval watched as his daughter knelt beside the pool ladder, plucking a small leaf from her foot and then tossing it aside. She didn't seem to notice the monkey as it charged toward her, teeth gnashing. Norval hurdled out of his seat, calling out to alert his daughter. But his cries were too late. Cassie's head lifted the moment the small primate was on top of her, its tiny body smashed against her like windblown paper smeared against a brick wall. Cassie cried out, toppling over as the monkey lunged at her before it tumbled from her shoulders and into the pool.

Norval helplessly watched the entire scene as if it were unfolding in slow motion. The vexed critter screeched before skittering away, frightened. Cassie lurched forward, unsteady, and skidded across the wooden deck surrounding the pool before she toppled over on her face. Some of the hotel guests milling about nearby saw the assault occur, women paling and some men intervening to help.

Norval sprinted across the deck toward his fallen daughter. She choked back quiet sobs, clutching her wounded foot. Several men in bathing shorts and floral shirts had already gathered around her, offering either their assistance or their concerns. Elbowing through the small crowd of onlookers, Norval came upon his daughter.

"The damn thing came out of nowhere," one of the guests said to his nearby wife.

"Is she bleeding?" a woman asked, pushing through the crowd.

Norval knelt beside his daughter, inspecting her leg. She winced, eyes watering, as his hands drew closer to her foot. It was then he noticed a large wooden sliver embedded in the bottom of her foot. He looked up, noticing one of the servers peeking his head over the throng of onlookers.

"Señor," he called out, waving to him. He figured he didn't have time to search for the Spanish word for "first aid kit." He just shouted the word in English at him. "Please. Hurry."

The waiter nodded, sprinting from the deck and into the hotel.

Norval wrapped his daughter's arm around his shoulder and gently lifted her to her feet, her body flinching slightly as she eased pressure on her wounded foot.

"Thank you, everyone," he said to the crowd gathered around them. "She should be fine."

The pack began to dissolve, couples returning to the comfort of their private curtained cabanas or wading back into the shallow end of the pool. Norval guided his limping daughter back to his table beneath the awning of greenery. Easing herself into a seat, she raked her head back against a cushion as Norval propped her leg up on a chair. He recoiled at the sight of his wounded daughter, unsure how to approach her, as if he were fearful of frightening away a small animal.

Kneeling beside her foot, Norval gently inspected the splinter. She winced, grimacing, as the sliver of broken wood stirred inside the tube of skin.

"Sorry," he said, recognizing her discomfort.

With trembling fingers, Norval tried to grasp the end of the splinter, but failed to make purchase of the tapered point as the sliver of wood crept further beneath his daughter's skin. Norval silently cursed himself. Not only for being unable to properly remedy Cassie's discomfort, but for how awkward and uncomfortable he was when tending to his child in general. Afraid to harm her any further than she had already been irreparably damaged, Norval cared for Cassie as if she were marked "Fragile, handle with care."

Just then, a dark shadow loomed over father and daughter, sunlight vanishing behind a tall shape as it towered over them. Norval lifted his eyes and was greeted by a row of white teeth, a single solid gold cap sparkling at him. Dressed entirely in emerald, the gentleman appeared so suddenly that Norval wondered if he had crawled out of the sprawling curtain of greenery surrounding them—the magnificently lavish inferno where flames burned emerald as grass.

"S'il vous plaît, Monsieur," the gentleman said, tipping his hat and revealing a halo of baldness in the center of his head so distinguished that it resembled a monk's tonsure. "I can be of assistance?"

Norval noticed the gentleman was clutching a small shoebox, bundled beneath his right arm as if it were a beloved pet. The hairs in his nose curled at the overwhelming scent of lavender as the gentleman drew closer.

"Very kind of you, sir," Norval said. "I've sent one of the servers for a first aid kit. They should be back soon."

The gentleman hooked the tip of his cane against the edge of the table, dragging an empty nearby chair closer to Norval and his daughter.

"Une absurdité totale, Monsieur," he said, leaning closer to examine the child's foot. "Dans les affaires de la santé, one can never be too careful."

Norval watched his daughter flinch slightly as the gentleman lifted her foot and inspected the splinter. The gentleman revealed a monocle hanging from around his neck and pressed the glass against his eye as he studied the small wound.

"Ah, voilà," he said. "Un monstre."

Norval cleared the catch in his throat. The only thing that made him more uneasy than tending to his daughter was watching someone else care for her.

"They should be back with the kit any minute now," he said.

"Oui. Bien sûr. But they won't have this," the gentleman said, revealing a small pair of tweezers from his breast pocket.

He brandished them in front of Cassie. Her eyes widened at the sight.

"Will it hurt?" she asked, her knees curling against her stomach, as if she were attempting to coil into a fetal position.

"Non, non, mon enfant," the gentleman promised. "It will be easy."

But, Cassie resisted, turning away.

"No. I don't want to," she said.

"S'il vous plaît, mon enfant," the gentleman said, his tone softening as if he were attempting to coax a small animal from the protection of its den. "We must do this. It might become infected. Unless you care for . . . amputation."

Cassie's eyes immediately snapped to her father at the word "amputation." For once, she looked as though she desperately needed him.

"He's only joking, Cass," Norval assured her.

81

"A splinter is no laughing matter," the gentleman said, straightening like an exposed python. "Especially here in the jungle when help is so far away."

Norval conceded the gentleman was right. After all, they were nearly seventy miles away from the nearest decent medical facility in San José. He recalled hearing stories of fellow travelers who were bitten by snakes or venomous insects while hiking and were barely able to be rescued in time. Most of their hiking guides had warned them to be extra diligent when hiking as a the slightest bite could prove fatal given the remoteness of their location and how inaccessible medical care was.

Of course, he knew full well a splinter may not pose a significant alarm at first, it was far better to be safe than to be sorry. Besides, he would never forgive himself if anything happened to her. He had made a promise to his wife as she accepted hospice treatment during her final stages of cancer; a promise that he would always care for Cassie no matter what.

"It's for the best, Cass," Norval said to her.

Cassie's shoulders dropped, her eyes lowering as if it were a sign of her finally giving in. The gentleman propped her foot on a small pillow, Cassie wincing as he moved her bruised leg. He prepared the tweezers for their labor, gently teasing the end of the splinter. Pushing the tweezers further inside her, he gripped hold of the splinter's point and dragged it out with one fierce yank. A tiny bubble of blood formed there, as if the small hole were now pouting at the sliver's absence.

"Et voilà," the gentleman said, glowing with pride as if more than satisfied with his victory. "A creature most horrible."

He brandished the wooden sliver—about the length of a cotton swab and just as thin—as if it were a living organism forever severed from its host.

"You'd like to keep it as a token of your ordeal peut-être, mon enfant," the gentleman said, presenting the splinter to Cassie on a cloth napkin. "After all, it could have been your leg, ma chérie."

Norval swiped the napkin from the gentleman's hands, easing the sliver into a small empty dish near his papers on the table. "Thank you, Monsieur. Very kind of you to help."

Almost immediately after, a waiter with a thin black moustache approached their table with a small auxiliary box with a red cross painted on its front.

"Señor," the waiter said, offering Norval the kit.

"Gracias, Señor," Norval replied, opening the kit and fishing inside for some cloth dressings.

"Any longer and we were considering amputation," the gentleman joked with the waiter.

The waiter, however, did not appear amused. In fact, to Norval, it looked as though the waiter and the gentleman had interacted before—a comfortability in their demeanor immediately shifting in one another's presence as if they were already well acquainted.

Norval couldn't explain it.

The waiter smiled politely and slinked away, unnoticed, as Norval continued to rummage through the small kit.

"S'il vous plaît, Monsieur," the gentleman said, interrupting Norval's frantic search. "If you'll allow me."

Norval passed the kit into the gentleman's hands and almost instantly the peculiar man located some fresh bandage.

"Now, we arrive at the fun part," the gentleman teased Cassie, unspooling the cloth dressing. "We mummify you."

With a flick of his wrist, the gentleman began to braid the dressings around Cassie's foot. Norval couldn't help but notice how carefree and joyful the gentleman was when interacting with his daughter.

It unnerved him.

But, more importantly, it made him jealous of the gentleman's natural father-like attentiveness.

When the gentleman was finished dressing Cassie's foot with bandage, he reached for the small shoebox he had set on the table.

"And for your bravery most extraordinaire, I have for you the gift," he said.

Tipping the shoebox in his direction, he lifted the lid slightly as if the precious contents of the box were a grave secret. Norval's face scrunched, quizzically studying the strange man as he peered inside the shoe box.

With a grand flourish, the gentleman revealed a small pair of leather woven shoes from the box.

"Un petit cadeaux," he said, offering the shoes to Cassie. "Something to better protect your feet."

The child didn't quite know how to react, at first searching her father for an explanation and a look of, "Should I accept?" Norval leaned back in his seat, unsure of the gentleman's offer. The gentleman seemed to immediately recognize Norval's distrust, straightening his posture as if in an attempt to appear with more formality.

"I couldn't help but notice your current footwear is less than agreeable for the jungle," he said, tipping his cane and motioning toward the well-worn pink flip-flops discarded beneath the table. "Now you won't have to worry about any other splinters."

Searching his mind for a proper semblance of gratitude, Norval intervened as politely as he could. "That's very kind of you, Monsieur. But, very unnecessary. Besides, they may not fit her."

"Size six and a half?" the gentleman asked, pushing the shoes toward Cassie as if insisting.

Cassie smiled, nodding.

"Voilà," the gentleman exclaimed. "I knew it."

Cassie took the shoes in her hands, admiring them. "Can I keep them?"

Norval softened, never wanting to disappoint his daughter. "If the gentleman says you can."

"They belonged to my daughter," the gentleman said with a maudlin look in his eyes. "I trust you'll take care of them."

Cassie nodded again, treasuring the leather shoes before slipping them beneath the table beside her flip-flops.

Norval thought it was odd, especially how the gentleman had referred to his daughter in the past tense. Of course, he didn't want to pry.

"Can I go play with the Cameron and Lacey?" Cassie asked, motioning to the Pruitt twins as they began to climb out of the pool and head for the vine-flanked pathway on the opposite side of the veranda leading to the nearby monkey sanctuary.

"As long as you keep out of the pool with those bandages," Norval said.

"Dad, I'm not an idiot," Cassie replied, springing out of her chair and limping after the girls.

"Mademoiselle," the gentleman called out.

Cassie turned, stopping in her tracks.

"Please to take care," he said, smiling.

Cassie nodded. She staggered from the table and eventually

caught up with the girls as they convened at the sanctuary's portico, and Cassie showed off her bandaged foot.

Left alone with the gentleman, Norval sensed himself shrinking—the threat of small-talk seeming almost unbearable.

"Well," he said, "thank you so much for your help."

"Pardonnez-moi, Monsieur," the gentleman said. "It was presumptuous in the extreme."

"No. Not at all."

Just then, a waiter approached the table with a silver platter carrying a glass containing black coffee as well as a sweating glass of ice cubes. He set down the glasses in front of Norval. Then, regarded the gentleman as if expectant.

"Señor?" he asked.

"Nothing for me," the gentleman said, waving him away.

The waiter bowed, retreating.

It was quiet between them for a moment, the afternoon heat hanging over the poolside veranda like an invisible net. The only noise came from the children splashing about in the water or the classic orchestral music playing softly from the small speakers hidden inside the surrounding lush greenery.

"Adrien Bouchard," the gentleman said to Norval, offering his hand.

"Norval Dowling."

They shook.

"Of course, you are American," Mr. Bouchard said, drawing out a cigarette from his breast pocket.

He tilted the small package at Norval, presenting him one. Norval politely waved the offering away.

"I can usually tell where someone's from before they even open their mouth," Mr. Bouchard said, sliding the filter between his lips and holding a lighter against the end. "One of my many talents."

Oh, God, Norval thought to himself. *Not another second of talking to this pompous ass. I can't take it.*

"Is that what you do for work?" Norval asked, spreading the sheets of paper out in front of him as if preparing an excuse to end the conversation and finally return to work.

"You could say that," Mr. Bouchard said, exhaling a thick wreath of smoke. "I collect things. Things people are usually unwilling to part with."

"I have an old armoire in my guest bedroom I'm dying to get rid of," Norval teased. "It's yours."

"Perhaps I will – ring you up – the next time I visit America," Mr. Bouchard said, lifting himself out of the chair and circling the table as he inhaled another drag.

Norval exhaled a sigh of relief.

Yes. Maybe he'll leave now, he thought to himself.

"You see, collecting things isn't my only specialty," Mr. Bouchard said, tapping the end of his cigarette into a small empty dish. "I've been endowed with other gifts as well."

Norval arched an eyebrow, about to invent some excuse to leave when Mr. Bouchard's eyes narrowed at him with dangerous intent.

"You see, I knew your daughter would fall and hurt herself," Mr. Bouchard said, his voice becoming brittle-thin. "I knew something terrible was to occur. I knew the moment I saw you. I only regret I wasn't able to prevent it from occurring."

Norval stirred in his chair, unsure how to react at first. "You . . . knew it would happen?"

"You don't believe me," Mr. Bouchard said, chuckling, as he took another drag from his cigarette. "My mother used to refer to it as la duexième vue. An ability to know certain things about people I shouldn't otherwise know."

"Clairvoyance."

"Précisément," Mr. Bouchard said, easing back into his chair. "I understand your skepticism."

"Well, of course, anyone could say they knew something was going to happen after the fact," Norval said, pouring some of the ice cubes into his cup of coffee.

"You must test me," Mr. Bouchard exclaimed, as if exhilarated by the prospect of a challenge.

Norval shook his head. "I wouldn't even know how or what to say."

"I'll help you, mon ami." Mr. Bouchard leaned forward in his seat, carefully studying Norval with eyes as narrow as a crocodile's. "For breakfast. You ate . . . one poached egg. And a grapefruit. Sliced four ways."

Norval let Mr. Bouchard's words hang in the air for a moment, not wanting to react. He needed time to think.

"Non?" Mr. Bouchard asked, prompting him.

"You could've easily seen me and my daughter dining in the hotel restaurant earlier today," Norval said, folding his arms.

"C'est vrai, Monsieur." Mr. Bouchard sat back in his chair, deflating slightly. "Perhaps another chance to prove myself?"

Norval said nothing. He merely uncrossed his arms, as if it were an approval.

Once again, Mr. Bouchard studied Norval with a scrupulous stare as if he were mentally vivisecting him.

"Your wife . . . passed away on December 12th," Mr. Bouchard said. "Three years ago, this December."

Norval was not convinced yet again. He glanced down at his arm, noticing the illustration of his wife visible beneath his shirt sleeve.

"You saw my tattoo and the inscription of the date she died," Norval said.

Mr. Bouchard merely smiled, as if silently coming to terms with the fact he will never sway Norval. "I suppose it's possible, Monsieur."

Mr. Bouchard rose from his seat, squishing the end of the cigarette into the small dish. He cleared his throat. "It's quite obvious you won't believe me. In that case, I will leave you to your writing your letter to Ali."

Norval looked up at him, his face whitening. Mouth hanging open, desperately trying to comprehend, he searched Mr. Bouchard for an explanation. His eyes glanced down at the sheets of paper scattered in front of him and then it came to him:

"You saw his name on one of the pieces of paper," Norval said, grinning as if he had caught him.

"Bien sûr, Monsieur," Mr. Bouchard said, circling the table the way a nighttime predator stalks their half-dead prey. "There's absolutely no way I could possibly know you avoid sleeping on your left side at night because it wears the heart out quicker according to an old movie you once saw."

Norval straightened, horrified at the realization.

How could he possibly know that? Norval asked himself, eyeing the peculiar gentleman as he paced in front of the vine-curtained terrace.

"I told you it was a gift," Mr. Bouchard said, picking up the green shoebox and tucking it beneath his arm. "Now, I want to be very clear. I don't want to leave any opportunity for vagueness.

Écoutez-vous?"

Norval slowly nodded, the sounds of children playing in the pool or other guests milling about dimming to a soft hum like a distant hive of honeybees.

"I had a vision yesterday when I first saw you and your daughter," Mr. Bouchard said, dragging a chair close to Norval's side and easing into the seat. "Now, there are two outcomes to this situation. I regret both are unfavorable to you."

Norval sat without movement, his eyes avoiding Mr. Bouchard's at all costs.

"The first scenario—your daughter will leave the hotel with me within the next hour. Her luggage packed and all of her things prepared," Mr. Bouchard said. "You will not intervene in any way. Nor will you alert the authorities."

A young couple, draped in damp towels, suddenly passed by the table and smiled at both Norval and Mr. Bouchard as they drifted by. Norval nodded politely at them while Mr. Bouchard flashed a grin so extravagant a door-to-door salesman might redden.

Once they had left, Mr. Bouchard resumed: "The second scenario—if you decide to interfere and keep your daughter from leaving with me, she will be bitten by a snake and die within the next hour."

Norval felt his chest tighten; his eyes remained trained on Cassie as she played with her friends across the way on the other side of the pool. His mind raced.

Surely, he can't be serious, he thought to himself.

Always one to steer away from confrontation, Norval began to collect his papers and stuffed them into the small rucksack he had set beneath the table.

"I think I've heard enough, Monsieur," he said, tightening his bag to close and tossing it over his shoulder. "Thank you for your help with the splinter."

But, before he could leave, Mr. Bouchard grabbed hold of Norval's arm and pulled him back.

"Pardonnez-moi, Monsieur," Mr. Bouchard said, his voice lowering as if his throat were filled with gravel. "It's of the gravest importance you listen to me. If you don't do as I say, your daughter will be bitten by a fer-de-lance viper. One of the most poisonous snakes in the world."

Norval resisted slightly, jerking his arm out of Mr. Bouchard's grasp. However, the old man did not retreat. Instead, he rose from his seat like an Emperor from his throne, sneering at Norval as if he were a mere peasant.

"I'm afraid you won't be spared either, Monsieur," Mr. Bouchard said. "You will be bitten as well. I'm pleased to report they'll be quick enough to save you from the same fate as your poor daughter, but not without severing your right arm."

"My right arm?"

"I'm afraid your tattoo will become a casualty, Monsieur," Mr. Bouchard said, plucking another cigarette from his breast pocket and lighting it. "Although you won't give it a second thought. Not while you're enduring the agony. I regret the matter affects me too. Comprenez? You see, if your daughter's bitten, I will also die a violent death at your hands. You will murder me."

Mr. Bouchard exhaled a plume of smoke directly into Norval's face, folding his arms.

"I've had enough of this," Norval said, swatting the smoke away and threatening to leave once more.

"My daughter and I vacationed here a year ago," Mr. Bouchard said, twisting the filter of the cigarette between his index finger and his thumb. His head lowered, eyes dimming as if recalling the unpleasantness of the memory. "She was bitten, too. I was with her when it happened. She lived in the agony for eleven minutes after it happened."

Norval swallowed hard. He tried moving, but it felt like his every extremity had hardened, as if bronzed.

Mr. Bouchard's eyes narrowed at Norval. "Are you so selfish, Monsieur?" he asked. "Are you willing to let your child suffer after knowing the kind of pain she'll endure?"

Norval's eyes lowered, glancing down at the table and noticing a small black fly floating in his half-melted glass of ice. The poor creature's tiny legs twitched as it tirelessly strained to crawl out of the water, but to no avail. Norval quietly wondered if the small insect could feel pain; if in its frantic desperation to escape a watery grave it sensed agony.

Before another moment of hesitation, he tipped the glass over and little cubes of ice spilled out onto the table like precious gemstones. The black fly launched from its prison, sailing into the air before fluttering away. Norval conceded if he could scarcely accept a mere insect's discomfort, his daughter's hardship would be completely unbearable.

He didn't want to ask it, but the words dripped from his mouth before he could stop them. "What are you going to do to her?"

Mr. Bouchard sighed, relaxed. "You mean to ask if I'll hurt her?"

Norval said nothing. His fists tightened.

Mr. Bouchard fished inside his pocket and pulled out a blurry Polaroid photograph. He regarded the picture for an instant, grinning. Then, he slid the image across the table. Norval picked up the photograph and was greeted by the blurred image of a woman—presumably in her mid-fifties, like Mr. Bouchard—outfitted in an expensive-looking ballgown and set amongst a throng of other distinguished party guests.

"My wife, Cora, and I will take care of her," Mr. Bouchard said, swiping the photograph away from Norval and pocketing it almost as immediately as he had produced it.

"You're married?"

Mr. Bouchard exhaled another plume of smoke, leaning back in his seat. "Thirty-seven years."

"She'll . . . be able to call her 'mother,'" Norval said.

He loathed to admit it, but he was seriously contemplating the thought.

"Naturellement," Mr. Bouchard said. "I would encourage it."

Norval worked over the scenario in his mind, beads of sweat creeping along the shelf of his upper lip. He knew full well Cassie needed a mother's love, and was more than certain that Ali, like him, would be a poor substitute for a maternal figure.

Without warning, a pair of shadows crossed over Norval and Mr. Bouchard like a dark curtain. Norval glanced up and was greeted by Eva Pruitt's effervescent smile, the string of pearls around her neck glinting in the sunlight as she drew closer to the table. Richard Pruitt—a man who insisted on wearing formal wear even in jungle heat—wrapped his arm around his wife's waist while twirling a tennis racket in his right hand.

"Enjoying your afternoon coffee?" Richard asked Norval.

Norval gulped uneasily as if the Pruitt's were unwelcomed visitors to a secret ritual between him and Mr. Bouchard—a deathly sacrament outsiders were not permitted to view.

"Yes. Very much," Norval said, grabbing the glass of ice he had spilled and correcting it.

It wasn't long before Norval noticed the Pruitt's glancing at Mr. Bouchard, as if expecting to be introduced.

"I'm sorry," Norval said. "This is Adrien Bouchard. We just met."

"Very nice to meet you," Richard said, offering his hand to Mr. Bouchard. They shook. "This is my wife, Eva," he said, pushing his wife toward Mr. Bouchard.

"How do you do?" she asked, shaking his hand and smiling.

"Pardonnez-moi," he said, craning his head around the Pruitt's as he glanced across the pool. "Are those charming twins your daughters?"

"Yes. Our girls, Cameron and Lacey," Richard said.

"You must to take care, Monsieur," Mr. Bouchard said, tapping out his cigarette in a small plate. "They will become a handful one day."

"They already are," Eva teased, waving at her daughters.

"We were hoping you might want to join us for a game of tennis," Richard said, brandishing his racket. "Mr. Bouchard is welcome to join."

Norval smeared the sweat dripping from across his forehead, wiping his hand on the handkerchief resting in his lap. "That's very kind of you to offer," he said. "But Cassie hurt her foot climbing out of the pool. Besides, Mr. Bouchard and I aren't finished discussing an important matter."

"That's alright," Richard said. "Perhaps tomorrow?"

Norval knew full well things would be different tomorrow. The last thing he would consider would be to play tennis. After all, it was very likely his life would forever change today under the skilled direction of Mr. Bouchard.

"Yes. Maybe," he said, his head lowering, knowing full well it wouldn't be possible no matter what.

"Well, alright then," Richard said, pulling his wife along. "We'd best get moving before the bugs eat us alive."

"Very nice to meet you," Eva said, affectionately touching Mr. Bouchard's shoulder.

The old man tipped his hat, nodding politely, as Richard and Eva drifted away toward the path leading to the tennis courts. When they were gone, Norval leaned across the table, eyes narrowing at Mr. Bouchard.

"Where are you going to take her?" he asked, a quiet part of him not wanting to actually know the answer.

"I've already made the arrangements for two first class tickets out of the country," Mr. Bouchard explained while admiring the luscious golden-brown bodies of young women and men reclining in the chairs beside the hotel pool. "She will have access to the finest education. An entire waitstaff at her disposal. Not to mention, a mother who will love her."

Norval's stomach curled. He could scarcely believe he was actually considering the man's offer. He had to concede access to a loving mother was not possible any longer if she remained with him. Perhaps once he may have been able to ignore his longing for men and agree to a rendezvous with a young lady so that Cassie might have a new mother. But not after he had met Ali. Not after his world had completely changed and he was free to be honest with himself and his desires.

"How do we arrange this?" he asked, loathing himself. "She may not go with you willingly."

"You agree to it, then?" Mr. Bouchard asked, straightening.

Norval merely nodded.

"Merveilleux," Mr. Bouchard said. "Now we must discuss the details of the transaction. A very important set of rules."

Norval could hardly believe this was happening, much less that he had willingly agreed to it. He wondered what his wife might think—how disappointed she would be with his care as a father. He wondered if perhaps she might prefer Cassie to find a suitable motherly replacement in her absence. Whatever the case may be, Norval could scarcely stop the transaction from happening now.

"You are not to make a scene during the hand-off," Mr. Bouchard explained. "You are merely to explain to your daughter that it's of the grave importance she leaves the hotel with me. That's all. You are not to say anything else. I will explain everything to her while we're en route to the airport. Comprenez?"

Norval imagined his daughter in the backseat of a taxicab, scared and confused—Mr. Bouchard, her only chaperone. Despite his queasiness, he silently agreed to Mr. Bouchard's instructions by nodding.

"Now, if you'd be kind enough to go inform your daughter of the change of plans," Mr. Bouchard said, drumming his fingers along the rim of the shoebox. "Our flight leaves at eight o'clock this evening."

Norval pulled himself out of his chair, staggering forward like a blind man as he began to make his way across the pool toward his daughter while she played with her friends. He felt like crawling out of his skin, somehow shrugging off his coat of flesh the way an insect molts its former self.

As he regarded his daughter, he considered his wife and what she might say—how horrified she would be of his decision. After all, he had made a promise to her to always take care of Cassie no matter what.

He knew full well this wasn't right.

He still had the chance to stop it.

"Mr. Bouchard," Norval said, turning. "I can't accept your offer. I won't."

Mr. Bouchard softened, as though he had been anticipating Norval's refusal. He reeled forward in his chair, snatching the shoebox from the table and rising to his feet. "And you're certain of your decision, Monsieur?"

"Yes. I am."

Mr. Bouchard's eyes lowered the same way a hospice nurse's might when addressing the family of a freshly deceased loved one.

"Très bien," he said.

Without hesitation, Mr. Bouchard tore the lid off the shoe box and revealed a small viper coiled inside. As if commanded by the sound of Mr. Bouchard's voice, the snake uncurled its slender caramel-colored body from peaceful rest and reared its glistening diamond-shaped head at Norval, hissing fiercely. Norval lurched back, crying out at the sight of the small creature. The old man shook the box at him, agitating the viper as it twisted in place and threatened to strike.

Thinking quickly, Norval lunged for the silverware on the table. He grabbed a dinner fork and with one powerful thrust to decide the matter he jammed the fork into Mr. Bouchard's face. The old man, stunned, staggered back while his knees buckled. As the shoebox toppled from his grasp, the viper leapt out and glued its mouth to Norval's right arm.

Norval flailed helplessly, screaming, as the viper clamped down and stabbed him with its fangs. Waving his arms in the air, the snake finally released him and was tossed into the nearby shrubbery where it slithered off, disappearing.

Norval watched as Mr. Bouchard tumbled back, hands swatting helplessly in the air before he finally landed on the small stone wall surrounding a nearby bed of flowers. His head smashed against the rock with a wet, cracking sound, his eyes fixed open and staring heavenward as blood leeched out like a dark shadow from underneath his head.

As strength abandoned him, all resolve leaking out from the two small puncture marks in his arm, Norval shrunk to both knees. A crowd began to gather around him and Mr. Bouchard's body, several men kneeling beside the old man and inspecting his lifeless body.

"Is he breathing?" one of them asked.

In a state of delirium—venom pulsing like an electrical current through him—Norval collapsed onto the deck, his body sprawled out like Mr. Bouchard's. More onlookers gathered around, kneeling beside him and inspecting the bite marks in his right arm.

"He's been bitten," one of the men shouted to the loitering wait staff. "Get a medic. Ambulancia."

Several members of the wait staff sprinted into the hotel lobby to call for help while others drew closer, carrying towels and pitchers of iced water.

Norval looked around, dazed, as he slipped in and out of consciousness. Without warning, his daughter appeared at his side, leaning over him as his eyelids mechanically open and closed.

"Cass," he exhaled, his every extremity softening as if his blood were warming like heated wax. "Don't go with him."

"Go with who, Dad?"

A server returned not long after, shoving through the crowd and coming upon Norval and his daughter kneeling beside him. "Help is on the way, Señor."

One of the gentlemen outfitted in swim shorts with a towel draped across his shoulder patted Norval on the shoulder. "An ambulance is coming," he said.

Just then, the waiter that had previously brought Norval the small auxiliary kit appeared at his side, his face as white as linen.

"Señor, I beg you to forgive me," the young man said, kneeling beside Norval.

Norval's head swiveled, his eyes glazing over. "Forgive you?"

"That man had paid me five thousand colones to copy the letter in your rucksack for him," the waiter explained. "I knew something bad was to happen."

Norval finally understood.

So, that's how the bastard knew everything about me, he thought to himself.

Suddenly, Cassie leapt up from beside her father and meandered through the small crowd toward the table. Norval strained to lift his head, his eyes following his daughter as she left him.

"Where are you going?" he asked her.

But several of the men urged him to remain still, pushing him back down to rest. Norval's eyes insisted on following his daughter as she craned her head beneath the table in search of her shoes. He watched as she uncovered them, sliding her right foot inside. Then, came the left foot. As soon as she shoved her foot inside the leather shoe, she lurched back and cried out.

Several members of the crowd swiveled their heads in her direction. Norval tried to sit up, but the pain radiating throughout his body was far too excruciating. He watched as some of the hotel wait staff sprinted to his daughter's rescue as she collapsed to the ground, crying.

"Cass," Norval shouted out, straining to lift himself up, but urged to rest by several of the gentlemen tending to him.

He watched as Cassie was comforted by several hotel staff members. As she cried, she pointed to her foot and it was there they saw two tiny beads of blood sprouting from between her toes. One of the wait staff members picked up the leather shoe Mr. Bouchard had given her, shook it gently, and watched as a viper slid out from its nesting place onto the deck and slithered off into the nearby underbrush.

Norval watched helplessly while servers tended to his daughter as she twitched, her eyes rolling to the back of her head. Then, he noticed his discarded rucksack droop into the pool, his handwritten sheets of paper addressed to Ali spilling out and floating across the water's surface like the downy feathers of a bird.

Glancing up at the vine-wrapped trelliswork above him, he watched as a monkey scampered from handle to handle. The small creature presided over the gruesome scene as if they were guests in his domain and he were their immortal deity.

I'LL BE GONE BY THEN

IT DOESN'T CREEP INTO MY mind the way it might for others who have known their mother all their life—a gentle realization of mortality when her hair begins to gray or when her hands start to prune with wrinkles.

It isn't delicately planted somewhere, like a beloved perennial to flower more amply each year until I realize the inevitable. No, instead it comes barreling into my thoughts like a home intruder; a masked assailant spraying the place with anthrax and laying carnage as I suddenly recognize the unavoidable: my mother is an affliction I wouldn't wish on anyone.

I make the horrible recognition as soon as one of the airport gate agents wheels her over to me while I wait at the baggage claim.

She's smaller than I remember from when I had seen her last. Although perhaps old age has robbed her of some of her stature, I can hardly recall such a loathsome scent shadowing her—a stench as vile as rotted flowers. I almost plug my nose, but I don't out of courtesy. Her skin is as transparent as parchment paper, her hair silky like cobweb. I notice her easily frowning mouth wrinkles slightly as she sees me, her lips puckering almost as if she recognizes me. I wonder if she does, but I'm answered immediately when her eyes begin to drift off and dim drowsily.

The gate agent flashes a hideous grin at me when she approaches, the imitation of joy etched into her face seeming to scream, "Please let this be over soon." She's dressed immaculately in a slim-fitted, powder blue pantsuit with a scarlet chiffon scarf draped around her neck like an open wound. As she approaches, grinning, I can't help but stifle a small laugh and wonder if her mouth hurts from smiling so unreservedly.

"Miss Vecoli?" the gate agent says, weaving through the crowd of passengers and finally arriving at me.

I slip my phone in my pocket and give her a halfhearted nod.

"Your mother was an absolute angel," she says, passing my mother's leather handbag to me. "Still a little sleepy from the flight. But we adored her."

"Is this it?" I ask, gesturing to the purse.

"Check Carousel Eight for any other bags," the gate agent says, already tiptoeing away from us. "Her flight from Rome was delayed a bit, but they should be delivering baggage there soon."

I search my mind, struggling to invent another question—anything to keep the young woman from leaving us. After all, once she leaves, the moment I've been dreading will finally arrive: my mother and I will be left alone.

"I was told she needed medication—?"

The gate agent is already backtracking and heading toward the escalator leading back to the main terminal. "Sorry. I wasn't told anything about meds."

Before I can utter another word, the gate agent climbs onto the escalator and disappears into the crowd.

It's finally here. The moment I've been quietly dreading for three months since my younger cousin in Vicenza phoned me at three in the morning, crying hysterically and apologizing that they could no longer care for my mother. It's an apology I certainly never deserved. After all, I'm the one who left Italy, abandoning my family in search of literary fame that never appeared even after nearly fifteen years of writing. Nearly two decades living in the States and I had a handful of literary magazine credits to my name, two maxed out credit cards, and an on-again, off-again liaison with a barista at one of my favorite local coffee shops.

I can't help but wonder if my mother still knew enough to resent me as she stirs slightly in her wheelchair. Whether her eyes avoid me out of spite or merely out of the disorientation that seems to cloud the elderly, I can't be certain.

Steeling my resolve, I kneel in front of her and place a hand on her lap.

"Hi, Mom," I whisper as if I were coaxing a fawn out of hiding. The word "mom" feels strange to say. "Did you have a good flight?"

My mother lifts her trembling head slightly to meet my gaze. I notice her eyes are dimmed and glassy like two small bowls of milk. Her lips quiver, as if trying to say something.

"A good flight?" I ask again, louder this time.

My mother lowers her head, eyes drifting as she stares off into the little crowd surrounding us.

"Sono stanco oggi," she says, her eyelids shrinking.

Even though I can understand what she says, it's something I don't care to encourage. I had left the language when I first abandoned my mother and father years ago. Even though the accent stalks me from time to time, I've done all I can to shrug off any indication of being a foreigner. I once read somewhere that people tend to not trust foreigners as eager as they trust their own kind.

I recall how an editor had once emailed me, telling me how he had adored the piece I had submitted, but that my surname was far too ethnic sounding to be included in his publication. That's why I've chosen to not only abandon the Italian language, but to also adopt a pen name. I had swiped at any opportunity to escape my past and yet here came a permanent reminder of everything I had tried to avoid, charging at me like a Gatling gun.

"Good flight?" I asked once more, as if hoping it might prompt her to respond in English.

She says nothing. Instead, she shrivels like a wreath of ivy abandoned in daylight.

I steer her toward Carousel 8 where we wait for the rest of her luggage. She dozes in and out of sleep like a drowsing toddler. I'll be damned if I'm going to wipe the saliva drooling from the corners of her lips. However, it's then I notice that people have begun to stare, children tugging on their mother's sleeves and pointing at the seemingly comatose woman. I fish in my handbag for a napkin and dab the threads of spittle trickling down my mother's chin.

After we collect her baggage from the carousel, I shepherd her from the terminal and into the nearby garage where I've parked my car. Once I've cleared the empty take out cartons and empty coffee cups from the passenger seat, I unstrap her from the wheelchair. She fusses quietly but doesn't seem to object to my manhandling. Loading her into the car like a bag of groceries, it feels strange to hold her as if she were a child. She squirms as I lift her from the chair and buckle her into the passenger seat.

We amble out of the parking garage and are on the highway heading toward Henley's Edge in a matter of seconds. I'm so absentminded I nearly forget my turn signal when changing lanes, and a middle-aged man wearing glasses driving a Subaru Outback glides past, flipping me off. My mother doesn't seem to notice. She's drifting in and out of sleep, her head lowered as if deep in prayer. I can't help but wonder if she still wears the same rosary pendant around her neck she wore when I was little—a necklace I once treasured unlike anything else and then quickly despised when I began to think for myself.

I wonder what's to be done with her—all the arrangements I'll need to make for her to live comfortably in the States with me now. I'll have to schedule a preliminary doctor appointment to assess her properly since my cousin was less than enthused with the doctor from Venice she had taken her to. I'll have to schedule a dentist appointment considering the fact that she probably hasn't been to the dentist in almost ten years. After my father had perished unexpectedly during oral surgery in his late eighties, my mother had been adamant about not regularly attending a dental hygienist despite my cousin's pleading.

Something will certainly need to be done about her clothes as all she seems to wear is expensive-looking black. Then, of course, there's the issue of her citizenship if she's to stay with me. Thankfully, my cousin did most of the legwork when acquiring my mother's visa to live with me. But now that she's here, I can't help but wonder if she's even coherent enough to apply for citizenship if it came to it.

People with brothers and sisters don't have to worry about these things. It's a shared burden between siblings; a mutual hardship as they inherit their parents' legacy. What exactly am I to inherit? A few measly rosary pendants and a trunk filled with clothing as foul-smelling as embalming fluid. Not to mention, the slew of debts trailing my mother and her deceased husband from when they rented an apartment in Padua. I had always thought parents were to open doors for their children. Mine couldn't even be bothered to open a window.

"Io ho fame adesso," my mother says, stirring from her sleep. Her voice is brittle-thin and damp-sounding as if fluid were collecting in her throat.

"In English, Mom," I remind her, gripping the steering wheel. My fingers flick the radio switch and music blares through the car speakers.

As we sail down the highway, the yellow arches for McDonald's drift into eyesight.

My mother points at them, her whole body straightening as if suddenly very much awake. "Cibo," she says. "Cibo."

I roll my eyes. I wonder if I should pretend I don't hear her— perhaps that might motivate her to speak English. After all, my cousin told me she was teaching my mother English words for when she was to eventually move here. Although she had only been quizzing her for three months, my mother had to have picked up on something.

I glance over in the passenger seat, and I notice my mother's attention glued to me, her eyes wet and shining. I certainly can't pretend I don't see her.

With a flick of my wrist, I nudge the turn signal and drift over into the exit lane. We drift down the rampway and meander into the McDonald's parking lot. I park near the trash cans and swing my arm over the seat to grab my purse.

"What would you like?" I ask her.

She doesn't answer. Her eyes are fixed on the teenagers skateboarding underneath the nearby streetlamp.

I nudge her again. "Mom. Food?"

She stirs slightly, her eyelids shrinking once more.

"I'll get you a burger and fries. A Coke to drink? OK?"

She doesn't respond, her mouth open and her breath gently whistling.

I fish my wallet out of my purse, haul myself out of my seat, and make my way into the restaurant. Even though it's mid-afternoon on a hot summer day, there's hardly anybody in the place. I'm about to go order my food when I realize I've left the windows of the car rolled up and the AC off. The dreadful thought suddenly dangles itself like a jeweled fishing lure in my mind—my poor mother will overheat and die. I imagine paramedics prying open the locked car door, my mother's sun-wizened body sliding out and splaying on the sidewalk. I imagine the scrutiny from strangers— "How could you leave the poor woman locked in a car on one of the hottest days of the year?"

I'm about to turn and sprint back out to the car to turn on the AC when I realize I'll no longer have to take care of her. She'll be a thing of the past, a distant memory. Of course, I'll have to handle a fair amount of scrutiny from the local authorities for leaving her in the car in the first place, but isn't the reward far greater than the adversity? It won't pain her. She'll merely fall asleep while death's fingers squeeze the life from her. She won't suffer. More importantly, I won't suffer.

The cashier's face scrunches at me, bewildered. "Did you want to place an order?"

I'm brought back to reality at the sound of her voice, my shoes squeaking on the linoleum tiles, and the overhead lights whirring at me.

"Sorry," I say, my cheeks heating red. "Yeah, I'm ready."

"For here or to go?" the cashier asks, her fingers flicking across the register's screen.

My eyes once again drift to my car parked beside the trash cans, my mother's head barely visible above the passenger head rest.

I return to the cashier. "For here," I say.

After the cashier slides a tray filled with a cheeseburger, a small carton of fries, and a large drink across the counter toward me, I make the trek over to the window overlooking the parking lot. I have a perfect view of my mother residing in her little tomb. I catch her reflection in the rearview mirror, her head lowered, and eyes closed like an abandoned marionette doll. She resembles an encaustic portrait of a martyr in the act of supplication—so gentle and so exposed.

I unwrap the burger and take a bite, imagining how it might feel for her when it happens. I wonder if she'll struggle, clawing at the door handle or beating her fists against the glass. Or perhaps she'll been swaddled in a blanket of heat and gently rocked to sleep. I wonder how long I'll have to wait for it to be over. Maybe thirty, forty minutes at the most. I certainly don't want to return to the car too soon and be greeted with a task I'll have to finish myself if she's only half-dead.

My mind begins to wander as I snack on a handful of fries, and I think about the moments we had shared when I was growing up. Tender moments outside of Holy Mass were few and far between, unfortunately. Quite suddenly I'm reminded of slicing pomegranates in our apartment kitchen while my mother brings a pot on the stove to a boil.

"Grenadine never tastes as sweet when you have to cut the pomegranates yourself," she used to say in Italian.

I was never allowed to have a taste as her homemade grenadine was usually paired with a fine liqueur after dinner; however, over the years, I've come to reflect on what she said. Essentially, it translates to "taking care of others is a thankless burden." I can't help but wonder if that's why the bitch had me cut the pomegranates in the first place.

Just then, as my eyes drift out the window, I notice a middle-aged couple swerve into the parking spot beside my car. The wife seems to be pointing at my mother as she dozes in the passenger seat, her husband nodding as if in agreement that they have to do something. They crawl out of their idling car and approach mine.

That's it.

I've been caught.

I swipe my wallet from the counter, knocking the food tray onto the floor. Fries scatter everywhere. I can't be bothered with that right now. I sail out of the restaurant and sprint across the parking lot toward my car. The husband notices me immediately.

"Is this your car?" he asks me, lifting his sunglasses.

I'm out of breath, trembling. "Yes. Sorry. I ran in quickly. Forgot to leave the car running."

"Yeah, we were going to call the police," the wife says, circling the car and cornering me.

"No, it's alright," I assure them. I press the key fob, unlocking the car, and climb into the driver's seat. "She's OK. Right, Mom?"

My mother says nothing, her face flushed.

The man circles in front of my car, his eyes scanning the license plate. "Are you sure?" he asks me.

"Yes. Fine," I say. "I'm sorry. We're late for an appointment."

I shove the keys into the ignition and twist, the engine

whirring alive. I'm backing out of the parking lot and veering onto the highway in a matter of seconds until the couple in the McDonald's parking lot are but a distant memory.

After the two-hour drive from the airport to Henley's Edge, we arrive at the small carriage house I've been renting on my landlord's property. As I lurch out of the driver's seat, I spy the remnants of the backyard swing set drowning in weeds behind my house—the place where my landlord's daughter used to play with her friends and remind me of the childhood I had robbed from me.

I haul my mother's wheelchair out of the trunk and prepare her throne. After I've finished loading her into her seat, I wheel her up the front pathway and steer her into the house. She doesn't seem to pay much attention to the papers scattered all over the floor or the half-eaten containers of Chinese food piled on top of one another. I notice her nostrils twitch, fingers plugging her nose at the stench waiting for us in the entryway. I had almost forgotten about the poor rodent that had met his untimely demise somewhere in the scaffolding behind the kitchenette.

"Sorry about the smell," I say to her. "Landlord's sending out pest control sometime next week to clean up the . . . remains."

There's a small, quiet part of me that hopes she won't be here next week.

Once I wheel her over to the window beside the couch, I clean the armchair of the bottles of soda and beer.

"If you'd like to sit," I say, gesturing to the empty seat.

My eyes suddenly dart to a pair of lavender-colored lace undergarments I had draped over the bathroom door. I snatch the underwear, tossing them into the nearby hamper.

I stare blankly at my mother, as if expecting some sort of penance for the ordeal in the McDonald's parking lot. She says nothing. In fact, she won't even look at me.

"I guess we'll order out for dinner," I say to her, shoving my hands in my pockets. "You still hungry?"

My mother's eyes close, as if distant and dreaming. She's probably lost somewhere in an insipid fantasy where she's accepting the Holy Eucharist from Christ, himself. I notice how her lips pout—her mouth like an untreated scar—as if she were being serenaded by a Requiem. There's no telling what's going on in her mind. After nearly fifteen years, it's like meeting her for the first time.

Part of me even wonders if she really is my mother, or rather if she's some monstrous creature wearing my mother's skin as a disguise. I think of pulling on her chin as if I were about to wrench away a mask of flesh and reveal a gruesome face pattered with blood beneath. I abandon the thought as quickly as it comes to me.

After we eat dinner in silence for what feels like hours, I show my mother to the sofa in the guest room where I explain she'll be sleeping until I can afford to buy a small bed. She looks at me with disappointment but doesn't say anything. Instead, my mother shuffles into the room and sits at the edge of the sofa, staring down at her patent leather shoes.

I watch her for a moment as if I were carefully studying an extinct animal. She'll never be happy here. I can't provide for her the way they're expecting me to. And why should I? It's not like she ever really took care of me.

I have to get rid of her. But how?

It's then I recall a news story I had seen printed in the local newspaper about a four-year-old who had been left by their mother at a laundromat a few towns over. The mother, probably unwed and young, was never heard from and couldn't be identified despite the authorities attempting to reunite mother and child. That's what I'll have to do. I'll have to leave her somewhere like a neglectful mother abandoning their child.

My mind races, imagining all the possible scenarios of somehow being reunited with her after I've left her. They can try to question her, but she can't speak English. Even if they brought in a specialist and he was able to communicate with her, she'd never be able to remember where I live. Then, I wonder if somehow they'll be able to trace her by her fingerprints. Yes, perhaps that's how they'll identify her. But what can I do? Burn each of her fingertips until they crisp black. No, I could never. I could barely stomach leaving her in a locked car in July heat. How could I possibly do physical harm to her?

They'll never be able to associate her with me. Even if they checked Italian dental records or fingerprints and finally identified her, they would never bring her back to me. I'll be long gone by then. Besides, I don't plan to waste away my life in

Henley's Edge forever.

They'll send her away to some nursing home where she'll live out the remainder of her days feeding on mashed potatoes and Jeopardy reruns.

It's then I make the decision—tomorrow morning after we have our breakfast, I'll take her to one of the parks in Hartford and leave her there.

I can hardly sleep at night. I imagine what it might feel like wheeling her to a secluded spot in the park, inventing some excuse to step away for a moment, and then never looking back. I wonder how long she'll sit there before she realizes I'm not returning. Maybe some good Samaritan will intervene, struggle to communicate with her before he telephones the authorities. Whatever the scenario might be, it won't be my problem any longer. I'll be gone and she'll be my gift, my burden, for the world to receive.

The following morning, I prepare some eggs and bacon. She doesn't eat. As usual, we don't speak. I go through her trunk and locate her capsule of pills, shoving them in her pocket.

"You'll need these," I remind her.

I'm not a monster. I'd never leave her stranded without her heart medication.

After I explain to her that we'll be taking a short trip to run an errand in Hartford, I steer her toward the car and load her inside. The hour-long drive there feels almost unbearable. The radio hisses the latest Top 40 hits, but I'm lost somewhere in my mind, inventing scenarios of how it might transpire—how somebody might see me with her and then come looking for me. What if they describe me to the police? What if they somehow connect me to her?

As quickly as these thoughts arrive, I shoo them away and turn the radio dial up higher. Finally, we arrive at the small park hidden just beyond the highway. There aren't many cars in the parking lot today and I quietly thank God for little mercies such as that.

I pile my mother into her wheelchair and maneuver her through the portico leading into the park. We drift by the fountain arranged at the entrance—a statue of some obscure New England patriot, sword unsheathed, as he charges into battle. We pass by the small lily pond, a few swans gliding across the mirrorlike surface. Eventually, we come to a small apron of greenery curtained from the remainder of the park by a column of well-groomed hedges.

"Let's sit here, mom," I suggest.

I wheel her beside the bench and kick the wheels so that they lock properly. We sit for fifteen or twenty minutes. Each moment that passes, I wonder if I'll finally get up and leave. Finally, the moment arrives. I can't bear it any longer.

"Mom, I'm going to find the ladies room," I say to her. "Wait here."

She doesn't respond. When she's not looking, I swipe her leather handbag from the wheelchair's handle and begin my way down the path away from her. My pace quickens as I steer through the hedges and, finally, she's out of eyesight. It's done. I've finally done it. She's gone—a mere memory as she was once before.

I wonder if she'll tremble with fear, wondering when I'll return. Maybe she'll try to come looking for me. It won't matter. I'll be gone by then.

I'm back at my car in a few minutes, hurling myself into the driver's seat and tossing my mother's leather handbag into the passenger seat. Just then, the bag spills onto the floor and something heavy rolls out. I peer over the center console and see it—a small pomegranate. There's a piece of paper attached to it.

I swipe the pomegranate from the car floor and peel open the small note. Written in my mother's cursive handwriting are the words, "For my darling daughter" scrawled in Italian. I sense my mouth hanging open, tears webbing in the corners of my eyes. I don't even bother to wonder how she managed to sneak the piece of fruit through airport customs. Instead, I crumple the note, slamming my fists against the car horn.

"Fuck," I scream until I'm hoarse.

Without another moment of hesitation, I leap out of the vehicle and make my way back into the park. Weaving through parents with strollers and young children playing games in the grass, I hurry down the path and toward the hedges where I've left my mother. I skirt around the corner of the shrubbery, and I see the empty park bench. My mother nowhere in sight.

My head swivels in every direction as I scan the nearby area. I don't see her. I don't even see the little indentations of the wheels of her wheelchair in the gravel where I had left her. It's as if she was never even there.

I notice a young couple approaching, and I ask them if they've seen an elderly woman in a wheelchair nearby. They offer apologies and explain they haven't. Once they leave, I approach a pair of middle-aged gentlemen playing chess beside the fountain. I ask them if they've seen my mother. They both shake their heads, bewildered by my inquiry.

I wander the park for an hour or so before finally giving up and going to the police station. I file a report and fill out all the necessary paperwork. I give them her passport, her birth certificate, everything I have in her wallet. They tell me all I can do is wait for a response. So, I wait by the phone for their call.

But they never do.

It's been nearly three weeks since I first lost her, and I've found comfort in few distractions. The nights are hardest when I invent horrible scenarios of what might have happened to her—how some leering predator might have spirited her away and drained her body until it was limp and bloodless. Or perhaps some kind, gentle soul had discovered her and took her in as if she were their own.

I can't decide which thought hurts more to think about.

During my days off, I visit the park and wander the hedge-flanked paths like a specter. I carry the small pomegranate so that if, by some miracle, I find her she's able to recognize me. Sometimes I stay until after sundown—until the sky is a black velvet curtain scabbed with specks of tinfoil—calling out to her and waiting for the dark to answer.

PLEASE LEAVE OR I'M GOING TO HURT YOU

IT'S CUSTOMARY WHEN HIKING—WHETHER it be the massive canyons of red clay out west or the pine scented trails of the Adirondacks back east—to greet fellow hikers with a cordial "Hello" when passing.

Everybody knows that. Even children.

It's one of those unwritten rules like shaking hands and making polite eye contact when you're first introduced to someone.

You can imagine my father's indignation when we were passed by not one, but two young couples in the span of ten minutes who had instead regarded us with the same quizzical looks of English settlers arriving in a virgin forest.

Or perhaps a more appropriate comparison is the same scrupulous looks of cruelty and fear the early settlers had shared with the land's primitive tribes before rejecting them, shepherding them by any means necessary—sometimes through unbridled violence—from the very seat of their birthright.

I soon realized their looks of bewilderment were not because we were busy gorging ourselves on a handful of wild mushrooms harvested from a small clearing not far from the trail. Nor were the looks of judgement a result of the unusualness of our attire—the both of us outfitted from head to toe in formal black as per my father's wishes despite the mid-July heat cooking us in the shade.

No, neither grievances gave the hikers trepidation while they passed us.

They were instead weary—perhaps disgusted even—at the sight of my eighty-five-year-old father and I holding hands, our fingers interlocked the way young lovers do. A momentary lapse in judgement, our eyes found one another and spiraled at the reminder—a poor habit yet to be broken.

We pulled our hands apart as the young couple passed us, our heads lowering as if in collective shame. But what exactly was there to be shameful for? A father holding his middle-aged son's hand? It wasn't as if my father and I had retreated to the nearby thicket, clothes being shucked, and body parts being oiled for insertion. It wasn't as if our naked bodies were piled on top of one another—a grotesque puzzle of human anatomy not even suitable for an Italian sculptor to solve. After all, some things are sacred in the privacy of a bedroom.

In the way a handshake is supposed to tell you the integrity of a man's character, there was much to be told in the stammering of words, in the awkwardness of lingering glances between me and my father.

There was much to be said in the way he lovingly adjusted my lapel for me when it became crooked, or the way in which I cleaned the dirt from his pants after he had had kneeled to collect the mushrooms for us to snack on as we walked.

It was always far more than the reverence a son has for his father—something that had been planted when I was very little but hadn't fully bloomed until not long after my mother had passed away two years ago.

Luckily, our guide, Mr. Turcotte of Carter Ridge Burial Plots, was instead far more alert to the surrounding wildlife than to his prospective clients.

"You'll notice some of these trees aren't native to this area," he said, gesturing to the nearby grove of white poplars. "Most of these were planted in the early eighteen-hundreds when this trail served as a railway line for the neighboring steel mills."

I glanced further down the tree-flanked corridor, sunlight trickling through the overhead canopy of trees and flickering at me like the headlight of a ghostly locomotive—hurtling toward me, its whistle shrieking, "Get out of the way before I hurt you."

That was perhaps the single most repeated phrase I had heard throughout the course of my life— "Please leave or I'm going to hurt you."

After all, it was the same thing my mother had said to me when the dementia had eaten away most of her brain. She had told me during one of her more lucid moments when she realized there were frequent moments when she no longer recognized me or her husband. Even worse, it was said to me by the only man I've ever loved aside from my father—a young waiter I had met while in college who had promised me a lifetime of happiness only to have it taken away when he had confessed to getting his ex-girlfriend pregnant.

The only person in my life who hadn't warned me, urging me to leave them, was my father. In fact, quite the contrary. He had urged me to stay, his neediness evident in the loving way he looked at me as I dressed him in the morning or washed him during his baths. Perhaps that's why I loved him—because he always needed me.

Even when I was a little boy with the yard work, we'd rake leaves together or burn piles of rotted wood in the backyard. My father never turned me away or even hinted at the thought of him hurting me. For him, it never seemed possible.

"How much further would you say?" my father asked, leaning against me for support. His pace had already slowed to a crawl.

"Yes. Maybe we should take a break." I braced my father with both arms, struggling to prop him up and peel the black blazer from his shoulders. "Dad, it's too hot to wear this. Why don't you take it off?"

But my father resisted, sliding his arms deeper into coat sleeves and careening further down the path. "Nonsense. I'm fine."

I watched as my father wiped a gnat glued to his forehead with sweat, his cheeks reddening with every labored breath he took. I shrugged at Mr. Turcotte the same way a parent might at another when their child throws a tantrum.

"Kind of a remote place to be buried," I said, shrugging out of my blazer and tossing it over my shoulder.

"It's picturesque," my father said, his head swiveling in every direction like a mesmerized child. "Quintessential New England."

"Are we even halfway there?" I asked Mr. Turcotte, patting the dampness from beneath both of my arms and wringing my sleeves to dry.

"Just a little further up ahead," he said, stopping to spray his exposed arms and knees with a can of bug spray he had been concealing in his back pocket.

It wasn't long before we reached a clearing where the pathway stretched to form a narrow causeway bordered by two large bodies of water—sprawling wetlands hidden behind colossal screens of greenery belting the path as if to prevent trespassers from wandering too freely. Bullfrogs secreted in their burrows or tucked beneath lily pads announced our arrival while small birds flitted overhead.

As we made our way down the narrow corridor, Mr. Turcotte gestured to small craters where the soil had been overturned and left on both sides of the causeway's embankment.

"Notice those?" he asked us. "Those are where the turtles laid their eggs in the springtime. Sometimes they get eaten by predators. But sometimes you'll see little prints of when they crawled from the nest into the water."

My father was on his knees in a matter of seconds, his hands carefully sifting through the dirt and scouring for evidence.

"I don't see any tracks," he said with all the disappointment of a child on the day following their birthday when the ribbons and balloons are taken down.

"Foxes tend to dig them up before they hatch," Mr. Turcotte said grimly, wincing at the unpleasantness of the thought—claws tearing through dirt, a thin snout foaming at the scent of freshly laid eggs.

Mr. Turcotte moved further down the path as if to escape the gruesome idea. But my father wouldn't budge from where he was kneeling no matter how many times I patted his shoulders. It was then I noticed he was holding the remnants of a small eggshell—freckled white—its casing split apart as if cracked by force.

"Do you think they hatched in time?" he asked me with the same panicked desperation I had only seen once before when my mother threatened to call the police because she didn't recognize me as she thought I was an intruder in the house.

My eyes fell to the eggshell remnants cupped in his liver-spot-dotted hands like the shattered bits of a gemstone. "I . . . don't know. It sounds like the predators often get to them first."

But my father was insistent. "Yes. But do you think they hatched in time?" he asked me again.

I wasn't sure.

I wasn't even thinking of the turtle eggs.

My mind was very much elsewhere, imagining how things might have been if my father and I weren't related—if we had met in his youth when his body was firm and when his mind was unclouded by age.

After all, age has a way of taxing the mind—as if it were a small penance each year for the cost of living—until we're a doomed specter of who we once were.

I recognized that my life would have been vastly different if I weren't related to the only man I've ever truly loved—the only man that's offered me the same amount of love in return.

"I'm not sure," I said, wishing I could do more to comfort him—perhaps a hand around his waist, the smallest and quietest of gestures to let him know he's cared for.

But I refrain from touching him, not because Mr. Turcotte was watching us, but rather because I'm afraid of overindulging.

"I hope they hatched," he said gently, tucking the eggshell inside his coat pocket and straightening until he was back on both feet. "I'd like to think they hatched."

My father was always optimistic that way—far more prone to compliment the preacher for the eloquence of his eulogy or the exquisiteness of the flowers decorating the casket as opposed to accepting condolences for his deceased wife. He'd sooner compliment than be complimented. Although it was a habit my mother often found fault with, I could never be persuaded to think ill of my father even when he was cross with me.

Looking back, perhaps that was the moment I should have told him—told him that I loved him, truly loved him, in the way my mother had once loved and cared for him. Perhaps I should have admitted to the scenarios I had invented in my mind—ideas of how our life might have been if we weren't related, mornings spent undressed and lazing in bed, afternoons by the beach reading to one another our favorite books by Russian authors.

However, I quickly realized Mr. Turcotte had ambled further up the path and was waiting for us. I wrapped an arm around my father and steered him away from the embankment, guiding him toward our patient trail guide.

After another five hundred yards or so, when the pathway veered into a thicket of towering pines, we came upon a stone wall bordering the left side of the trail. We meandered alongside the ribbon of stacked boulders before we came upon a small gate fastened shut with a latch rusted brown. Waiting beyond the gate on an acre of land were rows of headstones, some visibly newer and better cared for than others. Some were neatly shined and draped with bouquets of flowers, while others had been obviously neglected for years like the relics of deities from ancient civilizations no longer worshipped.

"Gentlemen," Mr. Turcotte said, unfastening the gate. "I give you Carter Ridge Cemetery. The only privately-owned cemetery in Henley's Edge."

We passed through the gate and we immediately began to weave through the rows of grave markers. My father, wide-eyed, searched the ground the same way a small woodland creature might explore a thicket for a new nest. He didn't even seem to notice my hand resting on his shoulder as we walked, far too entranced with the prospect of locating the place where he'll spend eternity.

"Where is it exactly?" my father asked, ducking down another row of headstones.

"Plot 72B just up ahead," Mr. Turcotte said, referring to his cellphone. "As well as Plot 86C next to the stone wall."

Finally, we came upon a small area of undisturbed land settled in between two neglected grave markers.

"This must be it," my father said, his feet springing up and down on the grass as if to test the ground. He looked around, admiring the scenery. "Beautiful surroundings."

"It's not like you'll be here to enjoy them," I reminded him. I quietly cursed myself for being so harsh, but it was the only coping mechanism I had to prevent him seeing me weakened at the reminder of the inevitability of his mortality.

"No," he said. "But you'll come to visit, and you can enjoy it."

His response perhaps wounded me even more than the thought of him dying—the unwaveringly cheerful attitude he possessed even when faced with his impending demise. After all, it was only a matter of time. He remained to be a man unlike any other—a bright candle with a flame dimming more and more every day.

I had known this man for my entire life—forty-three years— and I had never told him how much I had truly loved him, worshipped him even. It felt as if I had never even said "Hello" to him—I was no better than a stranger passing him on a mountain trail. I resolved myself to the fact that would all change today.

"Breathtaking views," my father said to Mr. Turcotte. "So peaceful."

"Your loved ones will relish in every opportunity to come and visit," Mr. Turcotte said.

Although my father looked as though he was ready and willing to sign whatever document Mr. Turcotte had prepared, I suggested we wait a day or so to consider all our options.

"Take as much time as you need," Mr. Turcotte said. "I'll have the papers waiting in my office."

"I think we'd like to stay and explore the area more," my father said.

"Of course. You can find your way back alright?"

After assuring him we'd be able to find our way back to where we began over a mile away, Mr. Turcotte closed the gate and headed off down the path and out of our eyesight. When I turned, I noticed my father a few headstones away, his fingers peeling some of the moss growing on the grave marker.

"You like this place?" I asked him.

But he didn't seem to hear me. He was far too preoccupied, his fingers squishing the bits of moss he had collected and his head lowering as if recognizing the very same decay will blanket him—the earth inheriting the traces of his legacy—in the not too distant future.

Once again, I tried to provoke him.

"Seems so out of the way," I said. "Plus, it's so close the marshlands."

"And that's such a bad thing?" he said, his fingers tracing the outline of the carved name in the face of the headstone.

115

I figured I might as well be honest with him. "I suppose I don't like the idea in general. You being here, I mean."

"You didn't have to join me," he said softly. "I could've done this on my own."

But his breathlessness seemed to say otherwise. I went to unbutton his blazer once more, but he jerked away from me as if insulted by the tenderness of my touch.

"It's too hot, Dad," I said, as if I had no ulterior motives in mind to undress him. "You'll overheat."

He was quick to change the subject, as if annoyed. "What do you think of it?"

I looked around, trying to imagine myself arriving to visit with a much more solemn expression, flowers in hand. "It's . . . beautiful, I suppose. But . . ."

I couldn't finish the sentence, the sound of my voice disintegrating like a thunderstorm breaking apart as it passes through mountains.

"Yes?"

I swallowed hard. "No place is good enough for you."

My father laughed, wiping some of the dampness from his brow. His voice slowed. "You care too much."

I wondered if this was my moment to finally tell him. But how?

"About you?" I asked. "Yes."

He patted me on the shoulder with a firmness all fathers are obliged to show their son's—the confidence in becoming a man. "You're a good son."

Before I knew it, the words blurted out from me: "I wish I wasn't."

He turned, as if he had misheard me. I notice his expression had soured, so I stammered for a moment before collecting myself.

"Your son I mean," I said.

Shit, I thought to myself. *That made it worse.*

"Then, it wouldn't be so hard for me . . . to feel the way I feel," I said. "About you."

I sensed my father drawing closer to me like a tick being drawn to the body heat of an animal.

"And how exactly do you feel?" he asked, cautious of each and every word as if they were dripping black with oil and needle-sharp.

"Like I can never have what I truly want," I said. "How I wish I had met you in another life so that things could be different for us."

My father merely blinked like a small cat communicating with its owner. I didn't need to spell it out for him. He already understood. I searched him for a reaction—a semblance of reciprocity, a gesture to signal his submission—anything. But it wasn't long before I realized I would go wanting for any sign of similar feelings on his end. There were none.

He didn't look at me with disgust but rather pity—unrestrained sorrow for the grown man confessing his love to him in the middle of a woodland cemetery.

"Have you told anyone else about this?" he asked me with danger residing in his tone.

I shook my head. I wouldn't dare tell him of the time my mother came upon me while I was pleasuring myself at the sight of their anniversary postcard sent from Vietnam. She died with that secret, the dementia leaking it from her memory like a faucet squeezing the remnants of her already half-melted brain.

"Good," he said, his eyes suddenly avoiding me. "I think you should go take a walk."

I started to inch closer to him, sensing the tether between us beginning to come undone as if it were a frayed wire. He stopped me before I could come any closer.

"Please leave," he said, "or I'm going to— do something I'm going to regret."

Without a second thought, I sprang from the cemetery and down the path until his threat could no longer chase me.

But was it a threat?

As my running slowed to a steady walk, I began to wonder if it was merely his way of saying he had felt the same way. It wasn't long before I came upon the marshes again, nearing the embankment where we had found the turtle nests. My eyes crept across the water, scouring the lily pads floating along the surface. Just as I turned to scale the ledge across from the embankment, I noticed a small eggshell tucked in the root of a plant near where the shore meets the water.

Kneeling, I gathered the eggshell in my hands. It was smooth to touch like a precious gemstone. I dug a hole in the causeway's ledge and a tiny crater yawned back at me as if it were a wound I had opened in the earth.

I pushed the egg inside, casketing it with dirt.

With it, I buried the longing I had felt for my father—the years of pining, the grief of telling him too late. Like a hatched turtle, these thoughts would eventually crawl back to the surface and make their frantic dash to the places in my mind where they once permanently resided. But, for now, they were buried—a beloved memory.

I waited an hour or so before returning to the cemetery to collect my father. When I arrived, I found what I had been dreading every morning when I would go to check on him in his bedroom.

I found him lying beside one of the grave markers, his arms neatly folded across his chest as if he had been formally arranged by an embalmer. His skin was as red and as shining as the infant petals of poison ivy—a bright crimson, only a ruby pendant could compare. The texture of his skin was no longer dewy but rather firm and taut as if all the sweat had been drained from him.

I pulled on his wrist—his skin warm to touch—feeling for a pulse only to be met with nothing. His eyes, practically dissolved pits of transparent gelatin, couldn't be wrenched from their stare at the sky above. His face, filled with color, aimed at the heavens as if he were contemplating his pathway there in his final moments.

I wondered if there had been panic for him—a desperate bargaining with an invisible deity before he had slipped away. However, the peacefulness of his composure, the softness of his complexion told to me it had been painless.

I quietly thanked God for that.

I reached into my father's pocket and retrieved the small, cracked eggshell he had taken earlier, carefully cupping it in my hands as if it were the only precious artifact I'll ever have to remember him. I squeezed the empty shell between my fingers until it shattered, dripping little broken bits down onto his body as if they were flower petals. Then, I laid beside him in the grass, swaddling him, as my hands pushed against his chest without a heartbeat—a reminder of what will never be.

I allowed my mind to wander, imagining the two of us as strangers in a bed somewhere, his body heat curling through me like a velvet gloved hand and a gentle voice whispering to me, "Don't leave. I won't hurt you."

Eric LaRocca is the author of several works of dark fiction and poetry including *Fanged Dandelion*, *Starving Ghosts in Every Thread*, and *Things Have Gotten Worse Since We Last Spoke*. Eric is represented by Ryan Lewis/Spin a Black Yarn for Film and Television. For more information, follow @ejlarocca on Twitter or visit ericlarocca.com.

CPSIA information can be obtained
at www.ICGtesting.com
Printed in the USA
LVHW010326011021
699202LV00003B/249